WHISKEYVILLE

When ramrod Trent Clanton quit the ranch in mid-round-up to attend an outlaw's burial in Whiskeyville, he wasn't looking for revenge. Sure, Burk Freemont had raised him and Horak the killer had cut him down. But nothing would bring wild Burk back now. Then Horak drilled another good man, kidnapping the post commander's wife and holding the army to ransom. Now, Trent Clanton had no choice. He buckled on his guns and took the vengeance trail . . .

RYAN BODIE

WHISKEYVILLE

Complete and Unabridged

LINFORD
Leicester

First published in Great Britain in 2004 by
Robert Hale Limited
London

First Linford Edition
published 2005
by arrangement with
Robert Hale Limited
London

British Library CIP Data

Bodie, Ryan
  Whiskeyville.—Large print ed.—
  Linford western library
  1. Western stories
  2. Large type books
  I. Title
  823.9'2 [F]

ISBN 1–84617–088–5

Published by
F. A. Thorpe (Publishing)
Anstey, Leicestershire

Set by Words & Graphics Ltd.
Anstey, Leicestershire
Printed and bound in Great Britain by
T. J. International Ltd., Padstow, Cornwall

This book is printed on acid-free paper

1

TWO FOR BOOTHILL

A high wind blew from the south-west, yellow and thick with flying sand that blurred the shapes of horses, cattle and men. It filled the day with the moaning of cedars, the complaining of cattle and the weary cursing of overworked riders. It hadn't let up for three whole days and nights.

The cowhands of the Strolling B ate sand at breakfast, noontide and supper, and when they crawled into their rolls at night, dog-tired with the ramrod's loud voice ringing in their ears, they slept with it all night long.

They hated it, the horses hated it and every half-wild beeve they managed to add to the gather was half-choked on it. This was a hell wind out of New Mexico to ruin tempers and bring on fights — all the more probable when hard-driving Trent Clanton happened to be ramrod.

'Loose them strings, O'Rourke!' he bawled at a puncher who was concentrating more on hunching his back against the duster than slapping a brand on a wild-eyed yearling.

The man obeyed and the steer jumped to its feet and trotted off to join the main bunch with a smoking new SBR etched into its red hide. The foreman grunted, eased his back to the wind and fished for the makings in his shirt-pocket.

Trent Clanton was twenty-five years of age, one of the youngest and toughest ramrods in the county. An inch or two under six feet in height, he was all bone, muscle and sinew, with a hard handsomeness about his bronzed features. The dust of the day coated faded jeans and hickory shirt, and the brim of his tugged-down black hat was chalky with the dried rime of sweat.

With a swift, practised motion he put

the cigarette to his lips, cupped a match in his hands and touched tobacco and paper into life.

Good — but not great. He doubted even a double slug of Old Magnolia bourbon would taste much better than linseed oil on a day like this.

His head jerked around sharply when the sounds of a sudden ruckus erupted over by the marshalling yards. When he saw the cause of the trouble, he flung the smoke away with yet another curse and wheeled the cow pony swiftly towards the commotion.

'Cooper!' he shouted, jerking the pony to a tail-sitting stop and jumping down. 'What the blue hell do you think you're doing there?'

Before the sweating puncher could reply the ramrod leapt down and reefed open the gate leading into the high-fenced corral. Inside, a longhorn bull was winning an uneven scrap with a stubby-horned shorthorn of about equal size. Skittish beeves were scuttling from the path of the antagonists. The shorthorn showed blood at shoulder and flank, slobber dripping from gaping jaws.

Clanton didn't hesitate.

He seized the longhorn by its horns and wrenched its head cruelly around. Sensing its advantage, the shorthorn recovered and charged. But Clanton was a veteran. He raised his right leg and timed his kick to perfection to catch the soft nose with a force that sent the critter spinning away with a sharp bellow of pain. The longhorn, still in his grip, tried to toss its head but he bore down on it and gave the neck a further agonizing tightening-up with a skill born of long practice.

'Get the tail!' he shouted to the group by the gate.

A Strolling B puncher rushed to obey. Grabbing the tail, he was able to twist it sharply and so steer the bull out through the gate. Immediately both men let go and the longhorn trotted off meekly to join the steers and bulls standing with their tails to the wind

4

against the fence of the long pen.

Clanton turned, slammed the gate to and slipped a rawhide loop over the post. They didn't like the way he looked as he turned swiftly with hands on hips to squint through the murk at the trio who were eying him warily; Danner, Silverstein and Bickner. They were new men, hired only at the beginning of the week by the Strolling B boss to help get the round-up finished after more men had quit. The trio had been giving Clanton even more trouble than the cattle. That was due to the fact that they'd come cheap, and rancher Buck Foster was a tightwad. Certainly Clanton demanded and got far above regular wages on the spread. But for that he was expected not only to boss a huge round-up but break in bums who wouldn't know a buffalo bull from a dogie weaner. He'd tried to be patient — but days and incidents like this would test a saint.

'Danner!' His voice cracked like a stockwhip. 'Is it true they call you crap-for-brains Cooper?'

Danner flushed and knuckled sand from his eyes. He was a meaty man with a thick waist that bulged over his gunbelt. He shot a sideways glance at Silverstein and Bickner before he replied.

'So I made a mistake, ramrod. Can't a man even do that in this outfit?'

'You've used up your supply, waddy.' Clanton jerked his jaw at the others. 'You all have. You're through.'

Work eased off around the yards. The regular Strolling B hands knew that that hands-on-hip stance usually meant trouble. Most liked Loner Clanton, but they always gave him plenty of room to move when in this kind of mood.

Silverstein paled. 'You're firing us, Clanton? Just for slipping a bull into the wrong pen?'

'That and another dozen other foul-ups — keerect.' Clanton jerked his head. 'Go draw your time.'

'The hell you say, Loner!' It was Cooper who spoke, Clanton who pivoted to stare coldly at the man. He didn't care for his nickname even if it might fit like a glove.

'Don't push it, Cooper.'

'Don't push it yourself,' the man fired back, big fists clenched. 'Foster hired us, he's the only one who can fire us. Ain't that so, boys?'

His sidekicks nodded vigorously, runty little Bickner actually moving deliberately to rest a hand on his sixgun handle.

Two things registered in Clanton's brain. One was that Bickner claimed to have some kind of gun rep in town. The other was that, on a day shaping up as the hottest of the spring, where there seemed to be more sand and dust in the sky than on the ground, and when he'd been dealing with proddy cattle, town-dumb hands and a slave-driving boss-man, he'd had enough.

He started towards Bickner. The man blinked, shot a glance at his companions then turned back to the ramrod only to find him almost on top of him.

Clanton struck.

The blow connected and Bickner's boots actually left ground as he sailed backwards to land on his back in a great cloud of dust, out to the world.

'Watch out, Trent!' came from the onlookers.

The warning wasn't necessary. The ramrod of Strolling B was in full figuring mode as he sidestepped Cooper's furious charge, then closed with Silverstein who landed one solid hit to his forehead before Clanton got his range.

Three lightning-fast straight punches put the beanpole down, and Clanton wasn't even breathing hard as he swung to face the real trouble.

Cooper came at him like an express train. The big man was fast and good. Clanton acknowledged both talents as he found himself staggering backwards from the effects of a vicious hook to the head that had him seeing stars. He was forced to back-pedal defensively as the brawler spun and stalked him with the intention of finishing him off.

It was in that split second, with the dust wind howling about him, goggle-eyed hands yelling encouragement from the background and his head still spinning, that the hard-driving ramrod of Strolling B realized that the time had come to quit.

It always came sooner or later, but he'd been on the Strolling B longer than anyplace he'd worked before and he'd actually believed at times that he might be actually settling down — at long last.

He ducked — and a whistling fist grazed the top of his head.

Seemed he would never get to settle, he brooded, as his head abruptly cleared, and he ducked another with ease. Ever since this orphan kid had graduated from the fetid crippled back alleys of Laredo he'd been endlessly working, searching, moving on. Now the wander bug was biting again — and the menacing figure before him had helped bring it on.

'Thanks, Cooper.'

'For what?'

'Never mind.'

He ducked low as the big fist came at him. He let Cooper crash into him harmlessly, then bobbed up and unleashed his favorite punch, a pistoning jab to the jaw that was followed up instantly by a breath-snapper to the kidneys, an elbow full in the face.

Cooper's eyes rolled in their sockets. He backpedalled but there was no escape. Unable to defend himself now, Cooper absorbed three blows to the jaw in as many seconds, and the ramrod stepped back to give him room to fall.

It was over.

Everything was over.

* * *

Muriel Foster saw the horseman approaching the headquarters as she stood by the scullery window, giving instructions to her cook. A plump and motherly woman of sixty who ran the great house seven days a week, and the Strolling B itself on those many days when her husband was absent, drinking or obsessing over cost-cutting and huge profits, she knew instantly that something was wrong, and her hand flew to her breast when she caught the look Trent Clanton shot in the direction of the house as he circled the pump and rode on towards the bunkhouse.

He was leaving.

She knew it because it was something she had feared every day, ever since the only man who could both run the Strolling B and work successfully with her difficult husband had signed on as ramrod just over a year ago.

'Oh, it just can't be, Gladys,' she cried to the cook. 'I must go talk to the boy . . . he's always liked me, I know.'

'Wish I could say he liked me.' Gladys sighed enviously. Then she sighed again and added: 'You might as well take him his letter if you're going over, Miz Foster.'

Muriel halted in the doorway. 'Letter? What letter?'

'The mailrider stopped by with this along with the paper while you were napping. It's there on the bureau.'

It was an ordinary-looking envelope, but for some reason which the maid didn't understand, Muriel's eyes lit up when she saw it.

'What wonderful timing,' she said mysteriously, and hurried off, leaving Gladys to gloom about what this place would be like if the best-looking cowboy in the county really did quit.

Clanton was emerging from his own room at the north end of the bunkhouse when Muriel arrived, all flushed and out of breath. He was stripped to the waist with a towel slung over his shoulder. He still appeared riled, yet some of the iron left his features upon confronting the only person 'Loner' Clanton had befriended here in over a year.

'Sorry, Muriel,' he said, 'but I've had enough.' He jerked a thumb over his shoulder. 'I told the boss and he's sore as hell. Then he offered to up my pay . . . that was before he threatened to horsewhip me . . . '

He broke off as the woman produced the letter from behind her back. Her eyes were sparkling, but she didn't say a word.

'Damn it, Muriel, what . . . ?'

Then he saw the bold handwriting and almost snatched the letter from her fingers, just as she knew he would. Muriel studied him eagerly as he ripped it open. His face was a study as he scanned the contents, first grinning, then chuckling, finally jumping down from the step to plant a big kiss on her honest cheek.

'Was I right, Trent?' she smiled. 'From your father?'

He was flushed with pleasure as he shook his head.

'Burk ain't my dad, Muriel.' He paused, then added with a distant look: 'Just the closest thing I'll ever have to one, is all . . . ' He glanced down to

13

scan the brief note again. 'Would you believe he's making this way and is fixing to stop by again.'

'I couldn't be happier, Trent. Then . . . then does that mean you won't be quitting after all?'

'Hell, no.' He laughed. 'Why would I want to quit?'

'I just couldn't imagine,' she said gratefully, then turned and hurried off leaving the most relaxed and cheerful-looking man on the whole spread to read his letter for the third time.

Burk must have known, he was thinking. He and the so-called outlaw from Whiskeyville had shared a rare kind of psychic bond ever since the long-ago day when Freemont had stumbled upon a ragged street urchin lying in a fetid back alley in Laredo, dying from pneumonia. But the kid had pulled through after Freemont got him to a doctor, and, even though they might only see one another every six months or so these days, they always kept in touch.

There was a spring in his step as Clanton went striding through the bunkhouse, between the beds, making for the washroom. The new hand who'd just arrived that day was perched on the end of his bunk, reading a newspaper. The man looked up and nodded to the ramrod. Trent had gone by before something caught the corner of his eye, caused him to prop and spin sharply.

'What is it, top?' the waddy wanted to know.

Slowly Clanton came back. The newspaper headline was in bold black type, and he'd caught the word 'Whiskeyville.'

He snatched the paper from the man's hands and read the blazing headline.

WHISKEYVILLE DUO DIE IN GUN BATTLE!

He felt his blood turn to ice as he forced his eyes drop to the next line:

Burk Freemont and Vic Wilson were yesterday . . . gunned down by persons unknown in the New . . . Limbo region in the wake of a brutal murder in . . . that town . . .

He was unaware of the paper falling to the floor. With a shaking hand he raised before his eyes the letter written by a dead man's hand — the best man who ever lived.

* * *

Five days earlier, the sandstorm approaching from New Mexico had been nothing but a faint upwards smudge on the south-western horizon as Horak idly watched smoke rise from his freshly lighted ciga-rette, the brim of his hat shielding his eyes from the afternoon sun. He had been waiting beneath a cottonwood in deep brush for half an hour — waiting for the gunmen. This was just a few miles out of the town where he'd left his bloody calling-card. A number of angry

16

men were out hunting for him but only two really wanted to find him.

His top lip curled in a sneer as he drew deep and listened to the sounds of crackling heat in the thickets. Just imagine two Whiskeyville fellow-citizens, Freemont and Wilson, sinking low enough to hire out to the Limbo Association — the fancy name for the small-ranch, no-money nobodies of Deaf Jones County — knowing full well that Horak and his side-kicks rode for the Association's enemies. To him, this amounted to treachery and would be treated as such.

He sneered contemptuously. If this was the best resistance the enemies of the cattle barons he rode for could throw up against them, then the small cattlemen were in even worse shape than he had figured.

A man would laugh if it wasn't so damn hot, or if he didn't have to keep real sharp. Freemont and Wilson might be growing long in the tooth but a man still shouldn't take them too lightly, he supposed. That sort of carelessness was how young badmen, like himself, didn't ever get to be old badmen, like them.

A lone eagle drifted overhead and the solitary figure watched it slowly disappear towards the west range. Far to the north-west on the fringes of the desert lay Fort Comstock. The broken blue line of the Panamint Hills formed the border between the semi-arid lands and the shimmering vastness of Spearhead Desert.

And roughly midway across that hundred-mile sweep of desolation, lying within the shadows of the Funeral Mountains, was the home of Kurt Horak and his fellow hellions, Whiskeyville.

He could make it home in two days. Providing, of course, that Freemont and Wilson proved smart enough to track him down quickly today, thereby enabling him to settle their differences quick and clean. Otherwise he might be obliged to go find the turncoats on what felt like the hottest day of the century.

Either way would suit; he really didn't care. He was riding a streak and nothing could stop him. He'd ghosted into Limbo last night on the trail of the Association's top man and was long gone and unscathed hours before the first possemen appeared out on the trails at first light.

He stubbed out the butt, tilted the hat over his face and leaned his back against the cottonwood, images of last night's savagery flickering beneath his closed eyelids like a gory magic lantern show . . .

★   ★   ★

Horak entered Limbo in the deepest night, the moon riding the south-eastern sky and the chill biting deep. He passed a drunk propping up a lamp-pole, the last defiant carouser in this shabby town's shut-down night.

'Hey, pal, got a quarter for a beer?'

the bum slurred — and the rider shook his head and tugged his hatbrim lower. It was vital that nobody realized Horak had come to town, it being widely known that he was currently working for either Moran or Quent, and both big ranchers were sworn enemies of the Limbo Association.

'Limbo for losers,' he mused as he glanced back to see that the drunk had tumbled over. Losers one and all. And tonight was Dunaway's night to lose big. Wim Dunaway had developed a big head and big ideas ever since grabbing the leadership of the Association. Thought he was really something after leading a bunch of small ranchers to clean up the rustler gangs who'd helped stock both Britten's Combine and Stillman's rival Big Six. They'd had other small successes while Britten and Stillman were busy fighting one another. But the heat had gone out of that rivalry, and the cattle giants had turned their attention to the troublesome Limbo Association, hence the killer's presence on that dusty town's hushed and shadowed streets tonight.

Horak checked his guns as the tall chestnut carried him past the beat-up general store. He wore a fringed buckskin shirt over faded Levis and straight-top leather boots handcrafted for him by a bootmaker in Nebraska. These were good boots with pointed, two-inch-high heels which enabled him to prop, pivot, spin or take off on any surface, including loose gravel or slick grass — handy in a gunfight at times.

Back then, when he bought the boots, he'd been just another outlaw, good with a gun. Now he was a big man with ambitions, and success tonight would take him higher up that ladder.

He moved steadily towards the central block, not knowing for sure where his man might be. He decided the hotel was the likeliest best bet.

He continued on quietly towards the narrow little unpainted hotel, squeezed in between the saloon and the feed barn, when a tight jerk on the reins brought his cayuse to a sudden stop.

The rider closed his eyes tightly for a long moment, then opened them again. This was always a good trick to enhance your vision at night. It worked for him now when he realized that what he'd only thought to be someone standing watch on the hotel gallery, turned out to be exactly that. A big man with a big rifle.

'Son of a gun!' he breathed almost admiringly. 'These poor bastards really are taking themselves serious.'

He eased into an alley and stepped down, allowing the reins to drop. No need to tie up, he decided. He needed the chestnut to be free, ready to run in an instant, which often in this game was all the time you had.

A stealthy shadow, he eased through the narrow back lanes that brought him out in the narrow space between saloon and hotel. The Cattleman's was only a six-roomer but you couldn't just go rattling from door to door searching for a grizzled nester with a big nose and notions above his station in life. He would need to see the register.

The rear door proved locked. Figured. Kurt Horak stood in the chilly dark practising his friendly grin before tracking up the side of the building to emerge up front not six feet from where the blocky figure with the rifle was seated on the edge of a plank bench.

'Howdy, pard,' he said amiably, stepping out into the thin moonlight. 'Know if they got any vacancies left in this roachtrap tonight?'

The man jumped erect, clutching the rifle. He'd been startled and was sore that he'd showed it.

'What . . . who . . . where the hell did you come from?' he sputtered.

Horak strolled to the steps and rested a hand on the rail.

'Horsehead,' he supplied, jerking a thumb. 'Heading for Richmond. Thought I might make her in one hit but me and my nag both petered out.' He was casually mounting the steps, smile fixed reassuringly in place. 'Didn't expect to find anyone up and about at this time . . . ' He halted as the muzzle touched his chest, feigned confusion. 'Why the shooter? What's going on here?'

Slowly the man lowered his weapon to make a closer inspection of this amiable-seeming nightcomer. It proved a huge mistake. Horak's right hand blurred. A .45 filled his hand and the barrel slashed across the sentry's forehead, cutting him to the bone. Strong hands seized the slumping body and dragged it into the shadows where it was let to slide to the floor.

He was inside in moments. A dim light burned at the scarred reception desk. He was leafing through the buckram-bound register when sounds of movement came from the hallway. Gun in hand, the nightcomer spun to confront a middle-aged man in pink long johns, holding a candle and blinking at him.

'Thought I heard somethin' . . . Who be you? Did Fallon let you in . . . ?'

It was Wim Dunaway.

Horak's gun crashed out and the figure was slammed back into the hallway, both hands clutched to his chest, falling with a great clatter of sound.

The noise barely carried to the killer's ears as he streaked through the open front door and cut left, powerful legs eating up distance in six-foot strides. The plan had been to kill Dunaway quietly and steal out the way he'd come in. But he could forget quiet now and concentrate on speed. His job was done — but he wasn't out of the woods yet.

Lights were blinking on and he heard doors and windows screech open as he swerved into the laneway. One leap took him into the saddle and he was on his way, bursting back into the street and leaning low over the horse's thick neck as spurs raked horsehide.

A cluster of men were milling about in the street by the hotel. A further two erupted from a building some distance ahead beneath one of the thorough-fare's only three streetlamps. Horak was vividly alert. From behind him the cry: 'He kilt Dunaway!' Ahead, the two men were now brandishing sixguns.

He cursed.

Freemont and Wilson, by God!

He'd known the Whiskeyville duo were working in the region but somehow hadn't figured on meeting up with them here.

'Judas bastards!' he shouted as he reefed on the reins to send the horse storming for the maw of the side street. He dimly heard a startled voice gasp 'Horak!' as the chestnut carried him swiftly away, the stutter of hoofbeats welling up against the buildings and drowning out everything else.

He burst into the open travelling at a flat gallop, and not even Freemont and Wilson dared come after him by night. But they would come.

★　★　★

Horak jerked alert.

The faint noise that stirred him from his reverie here in the brush thicket was caused by a hoof clipping stone. He was instantly on his feet and as alert as he'd ever been in his life.

If it proved to be anybody but Freemont and Wilson he would simply mount and mosey off. He'd done his job and had no interest in any small-time friends or citizens who might feel moved to come hunting for him. But Freemont and Wilson were cats of a different colour. The Whiskeyville pair had identified him on the street. They rode for Limbo and had come hunting him, which made them traitors in his mind, and that was a very different mind from most.

He was carefully brushing dust from his pants as a voice called:

'We'd better check out the brush. I'll take left, you right. Meet at yonder cottonwood.'

'Right. But I figure he's long gone, don't you?'

The reply was muffled, but Horak murmured, 'You hope, Wilson . . . you broken-down has-been.'

He set his hat at exactly the right angle, then shrugged his heavy shoulder muscles loose while cutting his eyes this way and that, a big bronzed man with a curious shambling grace. Well hidden, he was able to follow the progress of Wilson, coming in from the north, and Burk Freemont, now skirting the brush warily on the western side.

Backing up from the cottonwood, Horak angled away and eased south from the tree. The horse was tethered in a hollow 200 yards distant. It would make no sound no matter what. Neither would he. By the time he'd put fifty yards between himself and the cotton-wood he had both hunters to his north. He eased east a little, deciding to deal with Wilson first.

'Hey, Wilson!' a now invisible Free-mont hollered. 'You dragging the chain back there?'

'Keep your shirt on.' Wilson's voice

was thin and dry. He was scared, Horak thought contemptuously. He had every right to be.

Soon he was positioned in a draw directly below the animal pad that Vic Wilson was following through the brush. He deliberately moved into the open with his guns in their holsters, a smile puckering the corners of his mouth. He could see the long narrow face and bobbing shoulders of Wilson through the leaves now but the gunman was looking in the opposite direction. The man had his cutter in his right hand; his horse was sweating heavily. Wilson was mid-thirties and looked fifty. That was what the life could do to a man. Horak's contempt was absolute. Old, slow and riding for the wrong people. Three strikes and you're out.

'Howdy, Vic!' he called softly.

Wilson choked off a gasp and jerked on the reins as he saw Horak standing in the open below him in the full flood of afternoon sunlight. His gun began jerking upwards. It only had to rise inches to reach firing-level. But Horak drew and fired in the one fluent motion. Wilson's .45 tumbled from his hand and he stared stupidly down at his bloodied chest as he spilled from his saddle with the killer's Colts following him down.

He had four slugs in him but was still alive as he slammed the earth and rolled. That was how Horak sometimes did it. Inch by inch. The ashen-faced Wilson stared up in pain and feeble hope as the big figure loomed over him.

'For God's sake, Kurt . . . '

'I'm doing you a big favour, Vic,' he said, and shot him between the eyes.

A horse came crashing through the brush as the killer stood calmly reloading. He was looking down where blood was soaking the parched grass.

'Over here, Freemont!' he called. 'No need to hasten. I'll still be here.'

Burk Freemont was an outlaw who'd really been something in his prime. Cool and classy in any situation, he was still a top gun who knew exactly what he was up against right now. He feigned a pass on the left then jerked his horse right at the last moment to bring it racing along a line east of the big man's position. As Horak whirled smoothly to face the challenge, Freemont turned his mount broadside on and dropped down to fire from beneath the animal's sweating neck. The bullet whipped close, forcing Horak to hit ground, wiped away his smug smirk. Instantly his guns flared and the running bay was going down on its forelegs, the rider kicking clear a moment before it struck a tree. Freemont crashed against a stump, was stunned and hurt as he struggled to his feet, still with gun in hand. Coming up off the ground, Horak looked disappointed now, realizing how easy it was going to be after all.

'Come on, Burk, you can do better than this. Where's your pride, man? What happened to the Freemont men are always talking about? Am I going to have to just gun you down like an old hound dog whose time has come? Is that how it's got to be — pard?'

Freemont had a shirtful of agony. Busted ribs and internal bleeding, he diagnosed. He was staggering and groaning, yet suddenly snapped up straight and fast to touch off a lightning shot that just missed its target. Horak cursed and replied with a storming volley that dropped the man to his knees, fumbling with the gun that had saved the life of Burk Freemont a dozen times, a life now being brutally extinguished in the dust and blanketing heat of this nameless brushy hill.

'You are scum, Horak,' he gritted, struggling to lift the weapon with a broken arm. 'I'll be waitin' in hell for you, you miserable — '

Horak's guns spoke for the last time, and he left them where they lay to walk to his horse in the draw.

He pushed the chestnut west at first, towards the rangeland. The posse would chase him a little but not too far. He had blood leaking from a crease in the thigh, which meant he would have to take a long sweep round and stop by at Eagle Bluff on the way back to Whiskeyville. They had a doctor at the Bluff. He hoped he wouldn't be too drunk.

2

MAN ALONE

'Yes?' snapped the colonel, 'what is it now, Fisher?'

The corporal came into the office and snapped to attention with an exaggerated salute. 'Lieutenant Roades to see you, sir.'

'What about, damnit?'

Colonel Matthew Blake, commander of Fort Comstock, was seldom this taciturn or testy. But it had been a long hard day, as indeed most were this summer, and he was a weary man as sundown approached. The Indians with their complaints against the miners in the Panamints, the favour-seekers, the supplicants, the applicants and the simple time-wasters and professional petitioners were always with him. Yet the major problems these days were the rustling wars, which had flared afresh, particularly along the eastern rim of Spearhead Desert where the cattle monarchs ruled.

He'd had complainants of every stripe marching unendingly in and out on this ten-hour day and was in no mood for any further problems or issues, even if Roades might be one of his more favoured junior officers.

'Er, ah . . . the lieutenant didn't say, sir.'

The colonel pressed forefinger and thumb to the inner corners of his eyes. Tall and prematurely grey, the commanding officer of Fort Comstock was a no-nonsense officer who felt he was tiring badly towards the end of another interminable day.

'Of course,' he sighed. 'He wouldn't, would he?' He rose from his desk by the window, squared his shoulders and gave a curt nod. 'Very well, man, show the lieutenant in. And, Fisher . . . ?'

'Yessir?'

'I don't wish to audience one more

noble savage, one bellyaching nester or anyone who remotely resembles any kind of arms, beef or supply agent between now and the end of the month, understood?'

'Sir!' the corporal barked and hurried out. He knew his superior was just overworked and overstressed. The corporal hoped the lieutenant had some good news for him, maybe something not connected with the cattle wars.

That was a desperate hope.

For the harsh reality of the situation here was that the Army, specifically Colonel Matthew Blake's Fort Comstock command, located roughly halfway between the desert and the Indian country, was entirely responsible both for maintaining the peace and enforcing law and order. At present, the greatest threat to achieving these objectives was the outbreak of outlawry in the desert, which was somehow tied in with the ongoing war between the cattle barons.

Some days the colonel felt that he was secretly hoping that the sporadic

Indian troubles might erupt into a full uprising. Then he could go back to straight soldiering and leave piddling law-enforcement and general peace-keeping to those who should be handling it anyway.

The lieutenant entered, young, fresh-faced and eager, snapping a vigorous salute.

'Make it brief, Roades.'

'Brief it'll be, Colonel. Three men killed in Whiskeyville including Wim Dunaway along with two gunmen the Association recently assigned for his protection, Freemont and Wilson.'

'Damnation!'

'Sir?'

The colonel realized he needed a shot. Maybe two. But he never drank before sundown, he reminded himself. He was a man of disciplined habits who desperately missed his wife.

He straightened stiffly, hands locked behind his back.

'Talk,' he ordered in a calmer tone. He realized that the news just received was bad. As the newly elected leader of the small ranchers' association pitted against the major spreads far from the posts, it had seemed that Dunaway might succeed where others had failed.

Now the man was dead and there were bound to be repercussions, paybacks, upheavals, pleas for army intervention.

Lieutenant Roades heaved a gusty sigh.

'Whiskeyville involvement I'm afraid, Colonel. The worst — Horak. Shot Dunaway in Limbo, then killed Freemont and Wilson when they went hunting him.'

Blake cut his eyes to the Seth Thomas clock. 5.30. What time was sunset these days anyway?

'Horak,' he murmured, as though thinking aloud. 'Now which one is he . . . or are they all one and the same? Gascoigne, Hendry, Silver, Pedro, Stark? Why do their names stick in one's mind, when I wouldn't know one from the other, Lieutenant?'

'Perhaps because up here we only ever hear about them and never get to see them, Colonel.'

'Are we to believe that all this could be the work of Mr Moran and Mr Quent? This business of hiring butchers to kill other butchers, I mean?'

Blake paused at this point, his brow furrowing in genuine puzzlement.

'But the killers and the killed are all from Whiskeyville, you say? What sort of hellish community is that, anyway, where they will turn even on one another for the price of a drink? Even buzzards protect their own.'

'I'm afraid we know all too little about that hell-hole, sir. Seems we're always too busy maintaining peace in the Indian country and chasing rustlers here on the western side for us to pay much attention to the south and east.'

The fact that this was an accurate assessment of the Army's position in Deaf Jones County didn't help the colonel one bit. Blake's future vision for his command was one in which he would be totally atop all his problems in the region at any given time. Fanciful, of course. Currently he was barely able to control Indians and border raiders. This left little time or personnel left over to involve Fort Comstock in the ugly affairs of warring cattle kings.

'Well, thank you for brightening up my days, Roades,' he said drily. 'You may go.'

'Ahh ... any orders re the man Horak, Colonel?'

'What are you suggesting, sir? That I pull men away from Jehovah Canyon and the border in order to chase will-o'-the-wisps around that accursed desert?'

'Well, sir, this incident is bound to inflame the situation in the east county, and I thought — '

'That is what they pay me for. To think. And I think it's time you disappeared, mister.'

But Lieutenant Roades stanchly stood his ground.

'Begging your pardon, Colonel, but

there is another matter. Something I'm sure will offset this Limbo incident.' Smiling fatuously, he took a pink telegraph envelope from the breast-pocket of his tunic and proffered it. 'Communication from Mrs Blake, sir.'

Blake almost snatched the envelope. His fingers trembled a little as he stared down at it, not opening it yet. Cara had taken an extended vacation from the post to spend three months visiting with her family in Virginia. At least that had been her stated reason for her long absence from Comstock, although both understood that this was simply an excuse. They had not been getting along. Blake blamed the isolation and hardship, yet felt deep down that something far more serious was the root cause, perhaps something as serious as his younger wife not loving him any longer.

He had been writing to her, begging her to return. What if this message was just another play for time — or worse, a flat refusal? Then he realized Roades was fighting back a smile, and felt a quick surge of hope. He withdrew the slip and read:

TAKING TRAIN WEST TO PEARL CITY. PLEASE ARRANGE TRANSPORT FROM THERE. LOVE CARA.

Suddenly Colonel Blake felt ten feet tall, actually grinned at Roades, who beamed in response.

'I thought I should save the best news till last, Colonel.'

'You did the right thing, Lieutenant.' Blake re-read the message then looked up with a frown. 'Wonderful news but bad timing. Normally the only feasible route for my wife to make the coach trip from Pearl to the post would of course be via the north-west trail across the Hopi Hills. But the recent trouble between the miners and the Indians in the Hopis means I'd have to authorize a large escort to ensure Mrs Blake's safety . . . ' He moved to his wall map and studied it worriedly. Unfortunately

I can't spare that many men. So . . . I rather think her travelling quietly incognito by a different route would be prudent, given the prevailing unrest. Er, do you agree, Roades?'

Lieutenant 'Dusty' Roades blinked in astonishment to find his opinion on any topic being sought by the commandant. Yet when he saw the way Blake was looking at him, Roades felt a twinge of sympathy. For he was looking at a man who could lead a force of cavalrymen into a dangerous military action without a blink of uncertainty, yet who never seemed quite sure of himself where personal relations were concerned, especially in respect to his wife.

But Roades understood why the colonel was balking. The only possible alternative route to the Hopi Hills was Whiskeyville. He couldn't blame the man for balking at that.

'Whiskeyville should be perfectly safe if we arrange things carefully, sir,' he said, taking the burden of the decision from Blake's shoulders. 'Would you like me to work out the details of Mrs Blake's journey home, Colonel, you being so busy and all?'

'Much obliged, sir,' came the short reply. 'And, thank you.'

The colonel stood stiffly to attention until the lieutenant was gone before turning for the window.

Outside the fierce yellow sun blazed down over parade ground, supply stores, parapets and the fat black cannon squatting in their blocks, but Blake saw none of it. 'Mrs Blake's journey home,' Roades had said. He rolled the words around his tongue, savouring them. Yes, she was coming home where she belonged, perhaps for the last time, either to stay for ever or again to be driven away by whatever it was that was in him that had caused her to leave him before.

This time he would be different, he vowed. This time she would stay. She must. He'd never felt more resolute about anything in his life.

*   *   *

Trent Clanton woke at first light. For a moment he lay staring uncomprehendingly at the faded wallpaper of his hotel room.

Where were the unpainted bunkhouse walls and the cursing and groaning of half-wild cowboys struggling to get up and get to the cookhouse?

Then he remembered where he was and the day he had stretching ahead of him. He rose and dressed quickly, for the early-morning chill of the semi-arid lands was sharp in this nameless outpost on the plains of New Mexico, still many miles north-west of his destination.

He shaved and dressed by a window overlooking a rutted western street where a solitary early riser mooched by leading a tufted-eared mule, raising little puffs of dust.

Somewhere a rooster crowed raucously, but nothing answered. Could well be this was a one-rooster town, he mused as he knotted his bandanna. He might have smiled at the thought were he anyplace else, and had this been a different kind of journey.

The rectangle of fly-specked wall mirror reflected a very American face, square-jawed and short-nosed with a generous cut of a mouth and deep-set grey eyes. He set his hat on his head, then pulled on his shirt, faded crimson with a black armband pinned to the right sleeve.

Clanton had better shirts in his roll but this one was special. He called it his lucky shirt, although he wasn't expecting to encounter much in the way of luck on this journey to the Territory.

The hotel was stirring as he descended the creaking staircase, a rugged newcomer to these parts, dressed for the trail. Back in Kansas, Clanton rarely wore a gun, yet he sported a businesslike Colt .44 in a plain leather holster on his right hip today. Still with sixty miles riding ahead of him, he was already in bleak, sparsely settled country which would eventually deteriorate into the sprawling sweep of the alkali country beyond which lay the desert as one pushed further south-west. A man would be foolish to cross such country without a Colt. And a Winchester in the saddle scabbard, as well.

The 'hotel' comprised eight upstairs rooms, all featuring the same faded rose-pattern wallpaper, while the entire ground floor was a saloon, 'last one for sixty miles' as the proprietor had warned when he checked in last night.

It was shadowy and cool in the barroom and the scent of brewing coffee feathered his nostrils as Clanton strolled along the short passageway, bedroll over one shoulder, saddle-bags slung across the other.

The hook-nosed owner greeted him with a grin from behind the bar and invited him to join him for joe.

'I can fix you some breakfast if you're of a mind,' he offered. 'Not much of a cook, but I can fry a steak.'

'Coffee'll do fine,' Clanton said, dumping his gear on the bar. 'But you can let me have a bottle of rye and some of your cigars.'

The man nodded, studying the stalwart figure keenly as he filled the order. His gaze lingered on the crêpe armband. Nobody had mentioned it last night, but now he felt they were on familiar enough terms to voice his curiosity.

'Lose someone, did you, Mr Clanton?'

'Yeah.'

Just one word. It was enough to discourage the man from venturing further, but he figured destinations might prove a safe enough topic.

'Still figgerin' on makin' it to Whiskeyville in one day then?' he asked, slurping up his coffee.

Clanton tasted his own. It was surprisingly good. He said as much, then looked out through the doors at the desolate landscape.

'That's right. Got to be there by tomorrow.'

Funeral, thought the man. He would

imagine Whiskeyville would likely stage more funerals for a town its size than anyplace in the Territory. It seemed curiously apt that a town with its reputation lay almost in the shadows of the Funeral Mountains.

'Your hoss won't make it,' he stated like someone who knew. 'Not sixty miles this time of year.'

'I know. I plan to swap or buy a remount at that village on Council Creek they told me about last night.'

'Bunch of sly-dealin' no-accounts, them Creekers, pardner. Not out-and-out crooks or killers like they got at Whiskeyville, I don't mean, but shiftless and real shady.'

Clanton said wryly: 'Sounds like most of the horse-traders I deal with back in Kansas.'

'Iffen you don't mind my sayin' so, Mr Clanton, you just don't look like the sort of gent who should be goin' to Whiskeyville all on your lonesome, even if it is for a funeral.'

'No?' he drawled, sliding off the stool

and gathering up his gear. 'What sort of gent do I strike you as, friend?'

'What sort? Well, I guess I gotta say — clean-cut and hard-working, if I'm any judge. Sure, you look husky and capable. But Whiskeyville? Well . . . riding sixty miles in century heat to reach a rat-hole where they eat their own kind? I'd still think twice if I were you.'

Clanton laid a silver dollar on the counter.

'Good joe,' was all he said, then quit the room into the morning as the first hesitant rays of sunlight hazed weathered walls.

He couldn't help wondering what the atmosphere would be like back at the ranch. Buck Foster had been on the verge of apoplexy when he'd left. The man had tried threats, bribery, insults and cajolery to get him to change his mind about attending the funeral, all to no avail. Then, Foster-like, he'd gone crazy.

'You'll never get a ramrodding job on

any spread that can afford your thieving price as long as you live if you leave me in the lurch this way, bucko — a week short of finishing the round-up and with a two-hundred mile trail drive ahead. I'll see the Cattlemen's Association black-labels you from the Rio Grande to goddamn Montana, and don't think I ain't got the pull to do it, by God!' Then: 'Mother, talk to this ungrateful whelp, will you? He seems to listen to you, although God alone knows why!'

'Oh do quieten down, Buck Foster,' Muriel had said calmly, passing Clanton a food package she had personally put together. 'You know very well that by midnight tomorrow night you'll be crying drunk and praying Trent will forget all the stupid things you've been saying and come back and dig you out of the mess you'll get yourself into without him, just as sure as God made little green apples.'

He almost smiled as he stood on the stoop. Muriel had been right, of course.

He would be going back — and Buck would be in one hell of a fix. The smile faded as he glanced down at the armband. Losing a friend was hard on any man, but he had a hunch it mightn't be tougher on him than most. The reason for that was simple. Whether because of something in his makeup — or more likely due to the sheer brutality and loneliness of his childhood — the kid from the Laredo slums had grown to manhood mistrusting virtually everybody in his life except the unlikely Samaritan who'd once saved it.

Burk Freemont had been father, mother, brother, sister and pals, which meant they'd be burying all the 'family' he'd ever had when they dropped his casket into the desert earth of Whiskeyville.

He started for the stables.

The wind had eased off. It would be roaring hot by mid-morning and stay that way until nightfall. Sure, sixty miles was a hell of a push. But then, Burk Freemont had been one hell of a friend.

3

RATTLERS' NEST

The saloon man had seen it all, or so he claimed. There was no depth of human depravity any customer could display before the one-eyed proprietor of Whiskeyville's sole saloon that he had not encountered before — if you listened to him. Whether a man's weakness was lust, greed, violence, treachery or a secret plot to bring down the government of the United States, Gila always claimed to have seen worse.

Maybe he had, for when it came to hell-holes, Whiskeyville had to be in the first rank.

Bums and drifters and bleached-out whores patronized Gila's Bar on a daily basis, but the clients who'd made his place notorious across the Territory were the outlaws who found the town remote enough in Spearhead Desert to be safe for men of their breed; it was surely depraved enough to suit their low-grade tastes.

Sometimes an outlaw would be absent from Gila's town for months on end, but then he would suddenly reappear without a word and maybe just sit around drinking and gambling for months on end before disappearing once more.

Yes, they always came back to his saloon sooner or later, unless there was a .32 or .45 reason why they would never see Whiskeyville or anyplace else ever again.

Gila had been one of the hard ones himself once, a bandit and shootist until a job up in Colorado went sour and saw him fleeing from a bank when some old cracker with a .22 snapped off a shot that blew his eye right out of its socket and in doing so drained the last ounce of courage out of his once-fierce heart.

Now he supplied drinks both to

broken people like himself, as well as to genuine desperadoes such as he had once been, but never would be again.

'What'll it be, Jacko?' he asked his ragged customer, knowing damn well this wreck never drank anything but *aguardiente*, the pale, potent rum.

'Two fingers. Gonna be a hot one, Gila.'

'Is there any other kind, Jacko?'

It was Gila's indulgence to treat them with overt respect while holding all in private contempt. Being surrounded by misfits and failures made him feel superior, and he loved to see men and women exposed and fearful, their sins and weaknesses naked under his all-seeing eye while his own cowardice went largely unsuspected.

He poured red wine for the gaudy old trollop who lived in the loft over the stables, fixed Irish coffee for Mule Hendry and created one of his special headache potions for funereal Joachim Stark.

The latter pair were good spenders

and dangerous, men you could hire to beat up your wife, run a stage off a high trail or set your neighbour's spread afire with him securely locked inside.

Like the gunmen, outlaws and assorted riff-raff who called his watering-hole home between jobs, Hendry and Stark spent most of their time drinking, gambling, brawling and wenching, only occasionally vanishing, to be gone a few days or a few weeks, after which they might return, either flush again, shot to hell or sometimes both.

Just a handful were absent more than they were 'at home' in Whiskeyville. These were the top-notchers who hired out to the big spreads further east, fought their wars for them, stole cattle on order and helped keep going the feuds and rivalries that were so much a part of the real world beyond the desert.

'Anything on today, boys?' he enquired of Hendry and Stark as they drank quietly and thoughtfully.

Stark fingered his furrowed brow. The

big man had suffered crippling head-aches ever since they'd tried to lynch him in Cheyenne three years earlier. The frayed rope had eventually snapped but not before he had kicked and threshed for several minutes before blacking out for an hour. Brain-damage was Gila's gleeful diagnosis. Stark spent more on headache potions than most did on liquor.

'Guess we'll be stoppin' over until tomorrow,' Stark said at last.

'You mean ... ?' Gila began, and Mule Hendry nodded his bearded head.

'Yeah, for the plantin's.'

'The plantin's and the prayin's,' Stark expanded solemnly. 'If nobody else don't read over Freemont and Wilson then I'll sure volunteer. I've seen enough of jokers bein' shovelled into the dirt here without no mortal concern for their everlastin' souls to do me a lifetime. I mean, we might be scum, but that don't mean we ain't men, does it?'

Gila loved this. Now he had vicious

Stark fretting about the hereafter! What a fraud! If the man had been born with a soul it had surely shrivelled up and blown away years ago. Just like Freemont and Wilson. None of them worth one white dime!

'Here's to two good pards,' said Hendry, raising his glass. The man looked left and right before adding quietly, 'And it's a cryin' shame they had to die that way. Whiskeyville agin' Whiskeyville . . . bad, I say, real bad.'

'How do the rest of the boys feel about what happened up in Limbo?' he enquired soberly, smiling inside.

'Disappointed,' replied Hendry.

'Sore,' amended Stark.

'How sore?'

Gila wanted to draw them out on the subject of Freemont. For if this place had ever acknowledged one genuine hero it was him. And it was because of the man's popularity and style that he had hated his guts. He liked them broken and grovelling; the closer they came to resemble some kind of savage sub-human species the more likely he was to give them a little grudging credit. It was a safe bet that the late hero had been unaware of Gila's hostility, wouldn't have cared a cuss if he had been. For Burk Freemont, in the prime of his mid-forties, had been all style and personality. Tall, personable and great with a gun, he'd just wanted good times and excitement, the chance to earn a dollar and, of course, the opportunity to brag to anyone who would listen about his 'boy'.

Freemont had no offspring, but in his younger days he had been largely responsible for the rearing of an orphan kid he'd come across someplace in his travels, a very strange and unusual thing for any Whiskeyville hero to do, but then Burk Freemont had been different.

According to the late hardcase, his 'kid' had long gone on to do great things elsewhere, or at least so he always claimed. The town was aware that this surrogate son wrote to

Freemont regularly, which was more than could be said for most of the genuine offspring his Whiskeyville pards had scattered far and wide across New Mexico and beyond.

Gila was eager to discuss Freemont and how he'd died, but the hard faces opposite merely studied him soberly across the cedar bartop, silent and wary. Gila knew the reason for their reticence. Speaking out too freely about Freemont might be interpreted as criticism of Horak, and men were rarely sore enough or drunk enough to go that far at Gila's Bar. He read this in their faces, shrugged and moved along the bar to serve Johnny Silver, who never drank anything stronger than triple ryes before high noon, no matter what the occasion.

'Hot one,' remarked flashy Johnny, and a weighty, mid-morning silence descended upon the watering-hole as the climbing sun poured infinite fire down upon them from a shimmering sky, sending most of Whiskeyville's lost souls to seek the indoors to wait for the cool of nightfall however best they might.

The silence was deep, broken only occasionally by the sounds of hammer, saw or maul from the unpainted building next door which served as livery, feed barn, carpenter's shop and undertaker's. Where a pair of cheap pine boxes were being shaped to fit the mortal remains of two of the town's 'finest'.

While unnoticed, a bobbing black speck appeared far out along the faint trace of the south trail, slowly growing larger until it seemed to float like a leaf on a river in the rippling heat waves, eventually assuming the shape of a rider astride a high chestnut horse.

Gila was offering feigned sympathy to the late Vic Wilson's skinny, black-clad choppy from behind his bar when the saloon door banged open and Horak stood there with feet apart and hands on hips, wearing a brutally inappropriate grin. Gila shivered. Horak could have that effect on people who knew him well — especially those who knew him well.

'Please!' mocked the new arrival, holding up both hands, palms forward, as he entered. 'Hold down the applause, *amigos*. Could go to a man's head, you know, getting welcomed like a hero every time he gets back.'

The sarcasm sank without trace. The barroom remained silent and the new arrival found himself surrounded by blank expressions, averted faces, men and women suddenly preoccupied with their drinks, playing-cards, chips or fingernails.

All but Gila.

'You look like a man who could use a beer, Mr Horak,' he fawned, grabbing a bottle from beneath the bar. 'Warm enough, eh?'

Dusty and sun-browned, the big man came to the bar and grabbed the glass from the saloonman's nervous fingers.

'To Burk and Vic!' he shouted, holding the drink high. 'Went the way they wanted, standing up and shooting back. So, let's hear it.'

The killer was putting every drinker on the spot. Dour Wilson had been generally liked and respected, but charismatic Freemont had stood high. They knew the toast was mockery; how could it be anything else when Horak had cut the men down with his own guns? To support the toast would be to show contempt for the dead, as every man knew. This was an opportunity for every true friend of Freemont and Wilson to show his respect for the two and his contempt for their killer by the simple act of declining to raise his glass.

Not one man declined. Instead, every glass was lifted, every yellowback drinker responded:

'Freemont and Wilson!'

And Gila was thrilled to note that, no matter how low his customers might sink, they could always be relied upon to descend another rung lower. One day he might learn a better word than 'scum' to describe them fittingly.

Horak's disappointment showed plain. He'd arrived geared for trouble. He should have remembered there was rarely ever any hint of spark or spirit shown by nine out of ten denizens of Loser City.

But what about the others? he had to ask himself. The dangerous minority? There were cutthroats and backshooters and people who'd blown up trains and banks present here today. Men like Stark, Pedro, Hendry, Gascoigne, Dandy and Silver. Hard men all, and most had been on good terms with the dead. Surely you'd expect one of those to rise to his bait?

But none did or would.

People could say whatever they liked about Horak when he wasn't here; how nobody liked the big bastard and how while he was away you always picked up the latest newspaper hoping to read that they'd finally got him. But fear would always rule beneath Gila's high roof.

Mess with Horak even if he had just killed two 'good' men? Not a chance.

Cynical old Gila nodded sagely to himself as he watched the gunman tote his glass across to a table, where he sat with his back against the wall. There it was, he mused. Everyone in town hated Horak but none would ever challenge him, for nobody was that weary of life. But a man could day-dream, couldn't he?

Kill Horak . . .

The day must surely come when a man with guts and a gun would wait for Horak to come riding by on his tall chestnut, wearing his flat-brimmed black hat with silver conchos on the band. The waiting man, crouched and sweating, would wait until he was certain the horseman with the powerful build, the easy grace in the saddle and the iron features was indeed the one he was waiting for.

Then he would squeeze trigger and the last noise Horak would ever hear in life, as his whole body clenched tight as a closed fist, would be a firing-pin falling on a brass shell. He would feel the bullet ripping through his heart but never hear the shot that killed him.

Gila shuddered deliciously.

This was a good vision.

But in reality he had to wonder whether he would live to see Horak's last day. Or whether any of them would, for that matter. There were many here, particularly older folk, who honestly believed that which old Estralita, the crazy fortune teller, once claimed to have had revealed to her in an opium trance by one of her 'Cosmic Darklings'. She swore that it was written in her *The Great and Eternal Book of the Immortals*, that Horak would live for ever.

★　★　★

The girl looked up sharply. She was young, not yet seventeen, but full-breasted and knowing-looking. Her mother had been a Frenchwoman, married to a trapper working for the big fur brigades in Canada, and the Gallic strain showed clearly in the slant of her eyes and innate grace as she rose to arch her body and brush the hair from her eyes, eyes that suddenly widened with surprise despite her attempt to remain cool and unimpressed.

He was beautiful!

She could not recall thinking of any male in that way in too long. The men who peopled her village were rough and unbathed, often ugly and certainly never handsome. Riders drifted through from time to time, horse-dealers and outlaws and the like. They all stared at her in the same way, and staring back, she saw runts, beanpoles and men who looked like buffaloes trained to sit on a horse. But this stranger climbing down was rugged, bronzed and serious-looking, and she just knew he had the bluest eyes she'd seen all summer.

'Are you real?' she asked impishly. She half-expected him to snap his fingers and vanish in a puff of smoke, just another desert mirage.

'Real, dry and in need of a fresh horse,' he replied. 'I'm told you have horses here, Miss . . . ?'

'You can call me Amber. What are you called?'

'Trent Clanton.'

'So tell me, Trent Clanton,' she purred, circling him in a graceful feline way as she studied him at leisure from top to toe, 'what happened to you? Did you lose your compass, perhaps?'

'Huh?' Clanton was hot, sweating and in a hurry. Yet the girl was so unexpected in this dustbowl village, so full of animal grace and slinky charm — in her low-cut cotton dress cut just above narrow ankles — that he could feel himself relaxing. He was making good time. He'd make it to his destination on time providing he could do a deal on a remount.

She halted before him.

'I mean, of course, you must be lost. Yes, that can be the only explanation. Nobody who looks and talks like you ever comes here from one Thanksgiving to another.' She reached out to finger the soft material of his shirt. 'Tell me, lost rider, are you married?'

'Girl!'

The reproving bark came from the man who emerged from a nearby hut. He was fiftyish, unshaven, unwashed and smelt of whiskey and horses. It was her father, and he immediately sent her inside to make coffee for his 'customer'. As the girl had done, the horse-trader evaluated Clanton at a glance and decided he could only be a customer.

They haggled.

The dealer had horses for sale, trade or hire and was intent on taking his visitor for every cent. This didn't happen. Clanton knew more about horses and horse-trading than he did, and it quickly showed. He finished up trading his played-out horse for a remount of commensurate quality, plus five dollars to allow for the fact that his mount was now in poor condition at the end of a hard forty-mile ride.

'How come a young feller like you would use a horse up this way?' The man was sour and testy now, hated being bested.

'In a hurry,' Clanton grunted, saddling up.

'Nobody hurries in the desert. Too hot. Unless of course he's running from something.'

'I'm on my way to Whiskeyville, and there's a time factor.'

'Whiskeyville, you say?'

The man scratched his belly button through a hole in his stained singlet. Clanton didn't notice. He was watching the girl undulate barefoot across the hot earth carrying a steaming pannikin. A man could lose himself out here, he mused. Quit shaving. Start each day with a shot of tequila. Fight someone for a hot-bodied woman. Sleep all day and howl all night. Life could be that simple.

But not for him.

'That's right,' he affirmed, taking the coffee.

'They'll eat you alive down there.'

He cocked an eyebrow as he sipped. 'Who will?'

'Mister, it's plain you don't know beans about that helltown. I'm talking mean about the barbarians that live there. Lowest of the low, they'd shaft their own mothers for a dime. You look like dollars, and you're riding alone. Where do you want the body sent?'

'He exaggerates,' said the girl, watching him swing up. She shaded her eyes. Sitting his saddle against the burning sky, she thought he looked impossibly clean and heroic. She wanted to spring up behind him, twine her arms about his waist and bid him take her wherever he wanted to go. Instead she simply said:

'But take care, handsome one, even so. Will you return this way?'

'Could do,' he said, touched fingertips to hatbrim and heeled away, scattering chickens. He nodded in approval as his mount hit its stride, and called back: 'Good horse. Obliged.'

'Good horse, fool rider!' sneered the horse-trader. 'Whiskeyville! Lamb to the slaughter if you ask me.'

The girl could not take her eyes from the swiftly receding figure.

'You are an old man, yet you are not wise. That one is more than all those evil ones put together.'

'And how does a know-nothing female know that, I'd admire to know.'

'It's in his eyes and the way he carries himself. He is much of a man.' Amber touched her breast. 'I know it here. Any woman would.'

'What do you know about fixing a man something to eat?'

She didn't flare back as she often did. That would achieve nothing. The village was a prison where drudgery, habit and sameness were all one could expect and all you ever found. But the visit of the stranger had been like a message sent directly to her, reminding her there was something more out there, that she should never surrender the hope of finding something better. That man had given her that, just as a man named Freemont had once given the self-same thing to a homeless starving kid named Trent Clanton. So the world turned.

4

THE COLONEL'S WIFE

She sat alone in her plain hotel room with hands together in her lap and her face turned to the curtained window where the light had faded an hour before. Cara Blake was not strikingly pretty but had qualities that made her seem so. She could turn heads anywhere with her stately way of walking, the wide-spaced dark eyes and raven hair, a determined small chin. Too determined, or so her husband sometimes complained.

The colonel would prefer his wife to be more compliant, predictable and much more in keeping with the accepted perception of what a professional soldier's wife should be than young Mrs Blake was, or possibly ever might be.

74

The cold was seeping in already. The climate was just another element of the West she found difficult to adjust to. Summer days you roasted, summer nights you could freeze to death. A land of violent contrasts. But she would happily endure it all for the man she loved — providing he showed he still loved her. There had been faults on both sides; she knew that. Her principal shortcoming, as she saw it, was her romanticized view of what life could and should be in contrast to the way it really was. In her eyes, Matthew's was that he was a soldier twenty-four hours a day and did not even realize it.

Yet now she was going back. Back to the isolation and loneliness, back to her husband's bed after three long and exhilarating months in the East. Neither had put it into words but both knew this would be their last chance. Both wanted the union to succeed but there was no guarantee that it would or could.

Knuckles rapped the door.

'Supper's ready, ma'am.'

Cara rose with a frown. It still peeved her when men twenty years her senior addressed her in that formal way. Made her feel a hundred. She erased the frown as she got her shawl. She must remember not to act peeved, irritable, tetchy or testy, she reminded herself. That was how difficulties arose in a marriage. She would try to be calm, gracious and loving, and she could start off by not allowing her escorts to annoy her.

Sergeant Flint looked a stranger in mufti, a bulky man with an honest, ruddy face and a bad haircut. He escorted her formally along to the front room of the Pearl City rooming-house which stood along from the rail depot and where the colonel's wife and four-man escort had checked in. All five were now attired simply and soberly, with a drab-looking hired coach parked in the rear yard ready for tomorrow's journey.

The decision for the party to follow

Blake's instruction to travel west via Whiskeyville rather than the old miners' route across the Hopi Hills and Cross Junction had only been reached after long and careful discussion.

Whiskeyville was a stink in the nostrils throughout the region — but there were restless Indians in the Hopis. It was commonly known badmen lived in the shadow of the Funerals but desert-wise veterans such as Sergeant Flint were also aware that a large proportion of that outpost were drunks and bums who by and large posed no threat to anyone but themselves.

Cara knew her husband had recommended their taking the Whiskeyville track because he truly believed it to be the safer route. He was obsessive about her safety, and his judgement was rarely proven wrong, if ever.

A rancher with his wife and cowhands returning to their spread near Repentance via Whiskeyville. That would be their cover.

And Cara had to concede it seemed a

more acceptable way of her ultimately reaching the post with the minimum of fuss or risk, as opposed to travelling under full military escort and possibly attracting trouble.

She knew there were men who hated her husband for the inflexible way in which he maintained law and order, or at least how he strove to do so whenever he had the resources. Big men, bad men and little men with malice in their hearts. Any or all of them would hurt Matthew if they might, she knew, and some would surely not hesitate to hurt him through her, given half a chance.

Cara had confidence in the men assigned her, as she did in her ability successfully to act out her role as a rancher's dowdy wife. Indeed she felt almost excited at the prospect, and wondered what her stuffy friends and relatives back East would think if they could see her now, in her deliberately dowdy clothes, in rough company and considering a journey in disguise across a lawless desert. If only she could feel as confident about the outcome of their reunion, she mused.

Supper went a long way towards lifting Cara Blake's spirits again. The proprietors, a young couple who made her feel almost ancient, put on a fine meal comprising roast beef with greens followed by big platters of Richard's sourdough biscuits with an option of Sunday cobbler — cinnamon, sugar, sourdough starter, seedless raisins and a two-pound can of cherry-pie filling. The soldiers ate with the relish of men with months of unrelenting Army-post chow behind them, washing it down with good coffee and a port apiece. All five played their appointed roles quite convincingly, and Cara entertained with some stories of her recent visit back East.

The room was warm, almost stuffy. Outside, the Territory night was chilly as it always was after sundown. A fire had been set in the flagstone fire-place, dry shavings used to start up the heavy logs, until everyone had to move well back while the couple cleared away and one of the younger troopers began to yawn. Cara was listening to something the sergeant was saying about the Furnace Road, which they would be travelling to Whiskeyville, but had one ear cocked to the kitchen. The couple were working noisily and chatting animatedly, and once when she glanced out she saw him slip his arm about her waist and kiss her full on the mouth.

Later in bed, restless and sleepless, she thought about what she had heard, seen and felt between two normal people who simply loved one another, and felt desperately envious and deeply uneasy as a result.

Could Matthew and she ever hope to reach such a level of affection and naturalness?

She realized in that moment of true insight that it was not enough for her to be just a wife, she yearned to be a giving, passionate lover as well. And she sensed in her loneliness and doubt, with that mean night wind blowing sand against the windows, that in the end, irrevocably, she could never settle for less. At last she slipped off to sleep while praying that some miracle might change her husband into the lover of her dreams. The cold Territory wind seemed to chatter with mocking laughter at her womanly foolishness.

★ ★ ★

The undertaker-cum-liveryman and town carpenter drew back the canvas sheeting covering the body. Clanton winced when he saw how Burk Freemont had died. So many bullet holes. The corpse was bloodless, the final expression understandably one of agony.

'Well, you insisted on taking a look, sonny,' the man said, reading his expression. 'Seen enough?'

Clanton nodded and the cover was drawn back into place. The dead lay in their caskets in this back room behind the stables. It had gone nine and Whiskeyville was readying for the procession to set out along the dusty road for its already overcrowded boot hill.

Most newcomers were struck by the squalor and ugliness of this badlands sprawl of unpainted frames and mud huts which seemed to grow up out of the grey soil like warts on cowhide along the north bank of low-running Bobcat Creek.

Not Clanton. This was Laredo revisited. He sniffed and smelt decay. Everywhere you looked there was ugliness and depravity. It was like old home week. Then he thought about Burk, and shook his head sadly. Imagine a man of his calibre winding up here in his forties and still living dangerously, when by rights he should have been comfortably settled some-place far away and peaceful, maybe on a spread with his own small herd, wife and a couple of kids. The Burk Freemont he'd known had deserved one hell of a lot better than living and dying the way he had.

'Killed by a pal, you say?' he asked as he moved to the doorway.

'Guess that's just the luck of the draw in this town, son. Man hires out, he never knows who he'll come up against — '

'Feller named Horak, so I'm told,' Clanton interjected.

The man studied him, noting the breadth of shoulder, the upright carriage, the unfamiliarity of a male face unravaged by hatred, lust or depravity in this pest-hole he called home.

'I wouldn't get any foolish notions if I were you, mister,' he said warningly.

'Meaning?'

'Well, notions like looking to get square, mebbe.' The old man's gesture encompassed sagging barn, viciously rutted street, a straggle of watching men and women with finished faces, old before their time. 'Every man in town wears a gun and some are damn good with 'em. One or two are just plain lethal and Horak's about top of the heap. I wouldn't want to see you — '

'I'm no gunner.'

'So Burk always told us.'

'He did?'

'Sure. Hell, we 'uns here know just about everything about you there is to be knowed through Burk, young Clanton. Used to stand right there in my doorway reading your latest letter, so he did. I can see him now . . . ' A leathery smile split weathered features at a sudden recollection. 'Heck, he even used say he done his durndest to make a shootist out of his 'boy', only you was too smart for that. Claimed he was disappointed you never followed in his footsteps, but you could tell he was real proud. Everyone who's been around here a time knows you as 'Freemont's kid'. Did you know that?'

Clanton shook his head. He hadn't known. Yet it made him feel good. For if he'd ever been anybody's 'kid', it had been Burk Freemont's.

'Of course, looking at him now, young feller, you could argue you was right and he was wrong about how a man should live, huh?'

But Clanton's thoughts were elsewhere.

'I guess I can understand how men here could get to shooting one another. I'm just puzzled by all those bullet holes, is all.'

The undertaker's face puckered up until it was transformed into a distorted cross-hatching of wrinkles from which a big nose and beady eyes protruded.

'That's Kurt,' he conceded grimly. He turned his head and spat. 'Takes to killing as naturally like a duck to water, that one. Kills them by inches when he's in the mood or got the time. Heightens the pleasure, so he claims.'

Clanton went outside, where life moved sluggishly through the ugliest town he'd ever seen.

He watched a kid go by, bare-footed, hair in his eyes, wary.

The boy could have been himself

fifteen years ago. He'd been around ten when he first met Burk. Of course he would never know his real age, having been found in a basket left on a doorstep in Topeka.

The thing he remembered most clearly about childhood now was the hunger. Never enough to eat and always someone ready to fight you over what there was.

He half-grinned even though this was no day for smiling.

He'd learned to fight real good. In fact, he clearly remembered brawling with two much bigger kids in a laneway in Laredo, and whipping both, the very day before he took sick and came the closest he'd ever been to dying.

He would have perished but for the stylish stranger in a flashy suit with a big shiny gun in his holster who came swaggering past by purest chance, and got him to the medic just in time.

That was how it began.

This was where it ended.

★　★　★

The procession got under way an hour later, by which time the whole town knew that 'Freemont's kid' had shown up overnight to pay his respects.

Accepted as the closest thing Freemont might have had to real kin, Clanton was awarded the place of honour directly in back of the rickety cart carrying the caskets, along with a couple of painted women who fought all the long walk out over which of them Vic Wilson had really loved as opposed to just sleeping with when he felt like it.

The cortège was a strange one with derelicts walking side by side with hard-faced outlaws, slim-hipped gunmen arm-in-arm with saloon hustlers, a scatter of women of the respectable kind and a handful of kids trailing along behind, who seemed to regard the whole thing as a bit of a lark.

Even so, there was enough solemnity about it all to give Clanton the feeling he was laying his old friend away with just about the right mixture of warmth, sadness and respect. He spoke a few words, an alcoholic two-gunner read a passage from St Luke, and Wilson's whores delayed their inevitable brawl until everyone had returned to town and the wake got under way.

He alone lingered graveside to make his last farewell in private, was surprised at the words that came unbidden.

'Uncle Burk, would you believe that for the first time since you gave up on persuading me to follow in your footsteps, when I saw you laid out that way, I wanted to buckle on a gun and go after the man who did you that way. Bet that surprises you, huh? You always said I could make it with a gun, but I didn't have any killer in me. Well, for a few minutes there I felt could kill if I . . . ' He paused to grin.

'But it wouldn't surprise you to hear that the feeling was gone as fast as it came, would it? You always said the game would kill you one day, so I guess who and how you went isn't all that important now. *Vaya con Dios*, Burk . . . go with God.'

★ ★ ★

The one-eyed saloonkeeper showed quick interest when Clanton joined the wake at the saloon. Gila was unaccustomed to serving normal people across his bar, and for once was genuinely interested enough in a story to beg for more details on the bond that had linked the two men together.

'Nothing much to it,' Trent replied honestly. 'I was left an orphan, Burk helped rear me from a kid until I was old enough to look out for myself. He taught me how to use a gun and never to buy against an open-ended straight. He was the best man I ever knew.'

Gila's solitary eye blinked. He decided now he hated stories like this. He wanted to hear how someone had lived like a rabid dog, or how some bum had betrayed his best friends, his family and then his Creator before dying in disgrace with not even a little brown bat to mourn for him.

'He was nuts to get involved in that Limbo thing,' he said sourly, polishing his cedar bartop while temporary staff kept the drinks coming. 'But if he and Wilson were going to get involved, why sign up with the small fry? This is a big boys' deal. The big spreads, namely Moran's and Quent's, are going to end up with everything hereabouts in their big fat fists, maybe even get to mine the copper we all know is waiting up there in the Funerals just to be dug up whenever the Injuns move out. All the little men are going to miss out or, like in Dunaway's case, shot out of that game.' He nodded emphatically. 'Yessir, hiring out to the Limbo crowd was just plain dumb if you ask me.'

'Who's asking?'

Clanton turned to find Kurt Horak standing before him. The gunman was studying his reflection in the bar mirror as he hitched up his double gunrig. He was bronzed and brown, like a man carved from rock.

'Hey!' Horak said to his image. 'A man asks a simple question but nobody answers. How come?'

'We were just talking, Kurt,' said Gila with a worried glance at Trent. 'I was explaining what happened — '

'Dunaway and me had a difference of opinion,' Horak cut in, still not meeting Clanton's eye. 'He lost out. Then Wilson and Freemont made a Judas play and I paid them out for their trouble. What's to talk about?' He paused then added deliberately: 'Of course, that's unless anyone's sore about what happened?' The challenge lay there waiting to see if anyone wanted to take it up.

Clanton sipped his drink. It was true that Burk had taught him how to use a Colt, taught him well. He'd also taught him how to survive, drumming it into him from an early age that you didn't do so by responding to every challenge or taunt that might come your way, particularly so when outnumbered in strange country and surrounded by men who made their living by killing.

'Good enough,' Horak drawled, accepting his silence as submission. 'We got that cleared up.' He fixed Trent now with his iron eyes. 'But you and me ain't through yet, Freemont's pal. Let's talk out front away from the biggest ears in town.' He sneered. 'Big ears, one eye, no guts. But cheer up, Gila, we love you just the same.'

The sun had just set when the two emerged on to the saloon porch. Across the way, a woman in a red dress was spiking a downed drunk with her high-heeled shoes and screaming obscenities, above her the sky glowed with the flamboyant colours and delicate hues of a desert sundown.

'I'm not sure I'm buying your story, Clanton — if that's really your handle.'

'Why not? It's true.'

'Want to know something that's true? Sure you do. Well, the solemn god's honest truth of this Friday night is that your timing is bad. Matter of fact, it stinks. There are big things going on in the desert these days, just in case you don't know. I'm talking big plans and big men here, boy, and I'm up to the eyes in both. Lots of things have happened between men with a lot more cows than they can count and others who don't own a single one. There's land to be decided on, projects that'll take money to set up and will bring in more than most have ever seen. Some people are getting jittery and more men are going to die before it's all over. You following me what I'm saying — Freemont's boy?'

Trent didn't know what in hell the man was talking about. But one thing was clear. There was more to the episode that had cost Burk his life, and he had to stop and think whether he wanted to get involved in that or not. Losing your best friend was a hurting thing, and Trent Clanton had planned on quitting the Spearhead and going someplace alone for a few days to get his thinking straight before setting his jaw and going back to face Foster and the mess he knew he'd find on the Strolling B.

He'd reckoned without this man standing tall at his side.

He shouldn't have been surprised by the way cold rage had gripped his guts the moment he'd clapped eyes on the killer, knowing what he'd done, yet he was.

He was acting cool and rational, but that hot spirit that manifested itself on dusty hot days spent amongst bawling beeves and brawling men was stirring in a way that worried him.

This man had butchered Burk with viciousness and malice. But Burk had been hunting Horak, and would surely have killed him without hesitation had their positions been reversed.

Maybe cool and calm had to be the best way.

'More or less,' he replied, and the other nodded.

'That's close enough. The one thing

you got to understand is that right now, any stranger showing up here in the middle of these important matters might be some low life sonuva up to no good. You understand? You could be anything. Sure, I guess I believe you were Freemont's pal — he talked everyone blind about you often enough. But you also could be a Limbo spy working against me or the men I work for. That doesn't suit. That's why you're going to be on your way come sunrise. Understand what I'm saying — Freemont's kid?'

Again Horak hitched at his guns. He exuded power and confidence in this dying light. He was quite ready to kill if he must, and Trent knew it. And having already done what he'd come so many miles to do, he heard himself say:

'Tomorrow sounds OK to me.'

A powerful hand clapped his shoulder.

'Smarter than you look, cowboy.' And next moment he was alone under the dying skies with the night wind beginning to rustle in the chaparral.

He drained his glass and gazed off in the direction of boot hill. Burk would have to be proud of him right now, he mused. He was almost proud of himself, backing down that way. Trouble was, that for just a fleeting moment he'd felt a sudden, insane urge to pull his Colt and give Horak a quick six in the guts — ready or not. The 'killer' in him had raised its ugly head a second time in twenty-four hours.

* * *

Gila looked blank.

'Big doings and big men?' he queried, shaking his head. 'No, can't say I know anything about anything like that coming up here, Clanton. Who says so?'

'Horak.'

'Hmm.' Gila drummed fingers on bartop and looked thoughtful. Conscious of his self-image as the sage and all-knowing observer of Whiskeyville, he was reluctant to admit ignorance on any subject related to his town or its inhabitants. But in truth, he had no insider's knowledge of anything either major or new coming up for the desert hell-hole — at first. But he now realized Clanton's query was prompting him to recall certain details that just might mean something.

'Of course there's been plenty more coming and going than usual over recent weeks, what with the upsurge in rustling, the big ranchers getting grabby and the little guy fighting tooth and nail to hang on to what he's got . . . '

'You just mentioned the big outfits. That could be connected to the big doings and big men Horak hinted at.'

'Could do,' conceded Gila.

He broke off to serve two regulars, the broken-down former circus strong man who'd washed up here years ago and never moved on, and the young, half-wit girl who lived with him in a lean-to by the creek with a one-armed rustler neighbour one side and a two-bit shootist from West Virginia on the other. The couple moved off with their gins and Gila grew thoughtful again.

'Of course if big doings were in the air, Horak would have to be involved. It's no secret here that everybody hates that big 'un, but he's still *numero uno*, yessir. Fetches five times more in fees than guys like Hendry or Silver . . . ' His voice trailed off. He looked up. 'But how come you're interested, mister? You're not planning on staying on, are you?'

'No chance. Just curious, I guess.'

He strolled off through the smoky room, and here and there someone nodded, someone else offered a smile. He knew they weren't honouring him, but Burk. He was dead but he still walked tall in Whiskeyville.

He felt he could now understand how a congenial, rugged character like Burk would have found this place pretty much to his liking; enough work to keep him going, good pards, easy living and enough women to go round even if there had never been a special woman in his life.

He paused at the thought. Just like himself. Women, but no woman. Maybe he was more like Burk than he knew.

It was a bitch of a windy night outside now but he stepped out into it anyway, heading east along the main stem to take himself on what would likely be his one and only stroll around his friend's hometown, looking at the buildings and places that had meant something to him, saying goodbye as he'd been unable to do at the graveyard.

Unshaven men passed, bundled up against the night cold, some in horse blankets, a few in raggedy, flapping greatcoats of a style not sighted since the War. A high-breasted coloured woman switched by on snappy high heels, trawling for customers. Someone kicked a dog and a big-bellied man banged a drum on the gallery of the

Desert Heart saloon, inviting everyone in for a 'karmplamentry shart' of bourbon, which was in reality a blend of snakehead whiskey and hair-restorer with just a pinch of strychnine for kick.

At the edge of town he stopped to stare northward into the darkness of the haunted badlands. It was difficult to believe, inhaling dust and smelling the wild wind blowing in off vast regions of desolation and drought, that both to the north-east and north-west, within a hundred miles, lay green grass cattle empires supporting hundreds and even thousands of cows — along with big towns and railroads and booming progress — so violently in contrast with his surroundings that it was like being in another country.

He half-smiled at his own thoughts. Once Burk had chided him that he would never make a gunman because he thought too much. He was right. He'd become a cattleman instead, a good trade in which violent death and blood feuds played no part. And yet, standing there all alone in the vast cavern of the night with his face to a wind which carried all manner of stirring scents and fragrances, he felt just a twinge of that unfamiliar rage that had gripped him earlier on sighting Horak.

And wondered: if the boy who'd learned all about guns at Freemont's knee had chosen that route, where might he be now. Rich, famous, crippled or maybe dead. Well, he would never know and didn't wish to. *So long, Burk . . . hope there are plenty of good people where you've gone . . .*

The wailing wind boosted him back along the street. He walked with shoulders hunched and hat drawn on tight, hands thrust deep into his pockets as he realized he must have been out there much longer than he'd figured and the cold was really starting to bite.

It was with some surprise that, upon rounding the corner near Deane's Room and Board, he glimpsed the silhouette of a coach-and-four drawn up out front of the building with figures moving inside quickly out of the wind and cold, three or four men and one obviously a woman.

Somehow he didn't see this as the sort of place where travellers would want to stop over. He idly wondered if the party could be mourners arriving too late for the funerals, maybe even unknown friends of Freemont's he would like to meet. He went forward to find out.

5

KILL CRAZY

'What man in my position would ever want to set foot in a cesspool like Whiskeyville?' cattle king Hud Moran asked rhetorically. 'And not even his own mother would trust Clay Quent. So I'm being asked to get my ass into the saddle, ride all the way to that hellhole and actually sit down to parley with a son of a bitch who hates my guts almost as much as I hate his. That is Horak's solution? I always thought that gunhound was half smart at least, but this sure proves I was wrong. This only *proves* it. I'd be safer nightriding with you boneheads helping myself to Big Six cows like I've been doing for weeks now, and ducking Blake's troopers. I reckon I'd live longer. You tell me I wouldn't, gunrat.'

Vinnie Gascoigne, gunman and dude, was unperturbed by Moran's outburst. One of Whiskeyville's most dangerous and a current liegeman of Horak's in the range wars, he'd been selected by the killer to come visit both Moran and his rival Clay Quent whose giant outfits were located to the east of the desert in the buffalo-grass country. His task was to finalize arrangements for the planned meeting for the Mr Bigs in Whiskeyville.

Vinnie who had heard this sort of tirade from both cattle supremos before, refused to take it seriously. For it had been Moran himself who had first mooted the idea of some sort of Moran-Quent cease-fire and get-together. The cattleman's purpose in doing this was to minimize the costly fallout of the ongoing range war simmering between him and Quent, when both giants were already fighting the war on another front, namely against the scores of smaller outfits represented by the Limbo Association

Combine and largely supported by the Army.

The other reason for an armistice was far less well known, yet was possibly stronger. There were copper deposits deep in the Spearhead and each of the big men dreamed of getting his hands on them — if only the other would let him. Horak had laid down the groundwork for this meeting and had found Clay Quent suspicious yet amenable. Meet secretly on neutral ground under the protection of the gunmen and there, he hoped, iron out their differences and agree to work with one another and with Horak in a possible mining venture? Sounded risky but tempting to bulky Quent. But he wanted Moran to agree first, otherwise it was no go.

So Vinnie buffed his fingernails on his silk shirt-front and ogled Moran's young daughter and allowed the big man to rant on until he'd thrown up all the objections he could think of. Then Hud Moran dropped into an outsized chair and bent a fierce eye upon the hardcase.

'Well?' he barked, panting a little from his outburst. 'You're not saying much, mister. Is this what I'm paying you backshooters for? To sit around posing and smirking like damned popinjays? Is it?'

Smooth Vinnie Gascoigne had been a perfect choice to handle the final stages of the negotiations. He didn't turn a hair or betray any trace of offence as he rose and shot the girl a cheeky wink before responding.

'I'll take that as a yes, Mr Moran. So I'll be on my way to visit with Quent and set up the meeting in Whiskeyville for next Wednesday.'

The cattleman began to sputter but Vinnie cut him off sharply.

'Don't give me any more horseshit, Mr Moran. You know you want it, we're giving it to you, so why don't you cut the crap and tell me straight out to go tell Quent the thing is on. If not, mebbe I should cut north and tell Horak to drop the whole thing?'

Moran was startled. It was the first time any of the gunmen he was forced to deal with had stood up to him. It was all the more intimidating since Vinnie was usually so affable.

'I, ah . . . er . . . '

'That's definitely a yes,' the gunman rapped, heading for the door with cowboys staring at him popeyed. 'See you Wednesday, no ifs, buts or maybes. 'Night, Dolores.'

The girl blushed, Moran snorted and Vinnie was gone into the blustery night, hoofbeats fading swiftly into silence. Clay Quent would complain, demur and raise spurious objections exactly as Moran had done, he knew. But in the end he too would agree to what both desired so fiercely. Vinnie Gascoigne was very good at what he did, was almost as skilled at talking people round as putting them underneath the prairie grass.

* * *

The first rays of daylight were filtering through the chinks of the window-blind when the girl entered Horak's room. He stirred in the bed, undressed but for the .45 in his hand.

'Oh, it's you,' he said, slipping the piece into the gunrig hanging off the bedpost. 'Come here.'

He ripped off her thin cotton dress and she began on him with a long, hot kiss on the mouth with their bodies touching length to length, hers pressing against his, hot and soft under his hands. Soon she took her tongue out of his mouth and moved on down his chest and abdomen and lower, using her lips to kiss, touch and caress. She was highly skilled at what she did and soon he was responding with a raging hunger in the pit of his gut. He rolled her over and took her savagely. Her rising moans filled the room and he could feel her sharp nails raking his back as they continued until it was done and she was sobbing to God to forgive her. He was only half-way through his cigarette before he ordered her from his bed. She went meekly. Postplay and foreplay were never high on this man's agenda. Horak smoked his bitter cigarette through then got dressed quickly and took a look at the day.

'Another hot one coming up' could well be Whiskeyville's year-round weather forecast.

There was already heat in the sun as the Herculean figure quit the building to lean against a hitching post. His mood was reasonably good until he sighted the stranger moving along the walk opposite making for the roomer, and he remembered the unannounced coachload which had arrived overnight. The hostility and suspicion that characterized this man were back as he rolled another smoke and watched the stranger vanish down the side of Deane's Room and Board.

★　★　★

'More hotcakes, Miz Smith?' asked Momma Deane, plump cheeks flushed from the heat in her kitchen. The colonel's wife shook her head and stared steadily along the table at Trent Clanton as the woman scooped two more hotcakes on to his plate. Their glances met and Clanton was not quite sure what he said to Momma, something about more syrup or something equally banal. For some reason he wasn't concentrating, couldn't quite figure why.

Breakfast continued.

'Mrs Smith of Wildbreed Ranch and husband' had had sufficient, but guest Clanton and two of the couple's 'cowboys' were still doing justice to hotcakes and syrup washed down with what was by far the best coffee available in Whiskeyville.

Outside, life was stirring through dreary streets and dusty alleys. Already the blacksmith was hammering hot metal at his forge, the rhythm seeming to ring in time to the sound of hoofbeats raised by the lone rider coming in out of the desert.

'Mule Hendry,' identified Momma Deane, peering out. 'Lord alone knows what that one's been up to, and maybe a body's better off not knowing.'

The woman always acted alarmed and outraged by the outlaw culture that kept her town alive. Yet she had been in business here more than a decade and showed no sign of ever leaving. Secretly she loved the ongoing drama, confided to close friends that life in Whiskeyville reminded her of the Greek operas she loved, where sooner or later virtually everybody and his dog got wiped out, and the weeping and wailing never really stopped. The good lady found it virtually impossible to be bored here; the next atrocity was always just round the corner.

Yet for the moment, within the confines of the bright and cheery dining-room, with hardy flowers on the table and cooking-odours wafting in from the kitchen, Whiskeyville, in this early morning hour, could have been any peaceful town anyplace in the Territory, the sort of town where visitors might find themselves in no great hurry to leave.

Visitors just like Trent Clanton and the woman he knew as Mrs Smith, the rancher's wife.

But he was one visitor who was genuinely puzzled to find himself still here. Certainly when he'd met up with the coach party last night he was aware that the woman was highly attractive in a grave, almost sombre way and that he had gone out of his way to engage her in conversation, asking about her journey and her family while she seemed to return his interest.

And that seemed to be that — until he'd entered the dining-room to see her seated at the head of the table in a dark, plain dress with her hair loose to her shoulders, acknowledging his appearance with the smallest nod yet with something showing in her eyes, something he was still trying to define.

'We'd better not delay much longer, dear,' said Mr Smith.

'I know,' she replied. 'The heat . . . ' But she showed no sign of readying to go as she sipped what was left of her coffee and looked along the table over the rim of her flowered cup. 'I'm sorry to hear about your friend, Mr Clanton.'

Trent didn't know if she realized just what sort of town this was, but figured she must, living in this county.

He just nodded and said: 'Thank you, Ma'am. He was a good man but . . . but in the wrong business, I guess.'

'Most are down here,' weighed in the man named Smith with a heavy note of disapprobation. Then he rose and moved away from the table. 'I'll go help the boys fetch our gear from the rooms. Bob is seeing to the team.'

He left. Momma Deane turned from the door to find only Clanton and the woman left at the table now as the cowboys followed Smith out, still swallowing their hotcakes. The woman was about to leave. For some odd reason she had found herself reluctant to interrupt the couple's silence.

Clanton heard himself say abruptly: 'It's too bad you can't stay on a little.'

'Yes, that's what I think. Too bad . . . '

He listened to the beating of an ancient clock on the wall and realized that his confused reactions to this woman were at last beginning to clarify. He didn't want her to go because . . . because he didn't want her to go. It was that simple or that complicated.

He figured her to be a little older than himself, around thirty. More striking than pretty — apart from those grave, dark eyes which were her best feature — she carried herself in a way that seemed unconsciously regal. Her skin so pale, dark hair brushed until it shone. He was fascinated that this rancher's wife had hands as soft and elegant as an affluent lady of leisure. She raised her hand and pushed the heavy hair back from her cheek, in a gesture graceful and direct . . . and what the hell was really happening to him anyway? Trent Clanton, so he forcibly reminded himself, loved women and often pursued them. But he did not — he stalled at the thought — did not fall for them. In that way he was a loner, just like Freemont.

He rose suddenly and impatiently, ready to quit the room directly and go get his roll from the hotel.

Something held him.

He turned to find her eyes still gravely upon him, and found himself being drawn back to take the chair at her side, God alone knew why. Then she smiled as though he'd done something wonderful, and little else seemed to matter.

'More coffee, Trent? There's still some left in the pot, I think.'

'Coffee sounds just fine.'

* * *

The colonel had been in the saddle since long before daybreak. Not riding anyplace in particular, just putting distance behind him and savouring the wide open spaces of the lovely Indian country as he roughly followed a wide semi-circular route which would eventually take him back to the post.

He was peacefully all alone, while back at Fort Comstock his aides and officers would be chewing their nails and cursing his 'recklessness'. This solitary habit of his drove them crazy, and every time he absconded they reminded him of the dangers, specifically from the Indians but also from the outlaws, killers and all those Army-haters who drifted up from the deserts from time to time in sufficient numbers to warrant caution, especially for a high-ranking officer whose every action had such a profound effect upon the entire county. But he still did it because he needed to.

With the ongoing troubles involving the Apaches and the Navajo to the north requiring considerable Army involvement, the colonel was unable to direct the proper amount of men and resources to the upsurge of trouble in the Spearhead. His wife was still away, he felt like a desk soldier most of the time, and he went riding to ease his mind and to exercise his body in order to keep saddle-fit should the great day ever come when they might call upon him actually to lead men into battle and not just ride a padded chair.

But the thing that bothered him most today was the awareness that Cara and her escort were still travelling through the desert. The sergeant insisted they would be perfectly safe. The man had better be right about that.

* * *

Kurt Horak's eyes cut to mean slits as he picked a fragment of tobacco off his lower lip and stuck the cigarette between his teeth again.

'What's eatin' you, Kurt?' Stark wanted to know. 'What you staring at them stables for? Somethin' up?'

'Who travels this road, anyway?'

Sobersided Stark rubbed his mournful face, not understanding. As far as he was concerned this was just a quiet morning in town to savour before the big meeting between Moran and Quent took place in a day or two. There would be tension and full alert for them all then, keeping in mind how many little men had it in for the cattle kings and might try to get at them, despite the risk. But days like this, before the heat really hit and a man had the opportunity just to kill time and clean his shooters, were scarce and to be enjoyed in his opinion.

Plainly Horak saw it differently.

'Who are you talkin' about?' Stark wanted to know. His tone was careful. A number of men were working under Horak on behalf of Moran and Quent these days. All were beholden to him and were sensibly wary of the man. But none liked him, including Stark. Suddenly the man's eyebrows lifted at a thought. 'Hey, you mean Freemont's kid? Clanton?'

Horak spat tobacco again. This was one lousy cigarette.

'Freemont's kid! You crazy? What's to worry about a dumb cowpuncher? I'm talking about them that showed last night. The hick farmer and his bunch. Or so he says he is. They are still here, yet they said last night they'd be off and away early. Think of it, Stark. Four geezers, respectable-looking ones too, when you look at them. From a spread we never heard of, and taking the Furnace Road to boot. All this going on with the big powwow just round the corner? I smell fish.'

Joachim Stark sighed noisily. It was never easy working with Horak. He always had you on your toes for one reason or another. Yet he had to concede that, more often than not when Kurt Horak scented fish, a flathead or catfish seemed to turn up somewhere close about.

Stark was sober as he stared across at

the hotel stables.

'You're thinkin' they could be Combine men lookin' to make trouble?'

'Only one way to find out, sobersides. Keep a watch from here. I see a geezer inside harnessing the horses. Him and me are going to talk.'

Stark sighed again as he drew his revolver from its holster and slipped it behind his studded belt buckle. Often when Horak went 'talking' it could end up ugly.

The stables were cool and gloomy. Despite his bulk, Horak entered without a sound. The husky young traveller was lifting harness down off a saddle tree. He started when the voice sounded right behind.

'Let's see some documents, pilgrim.'

The man whirled. He was a corporal in the US Cavalry. He did not scare easily, but he recognized danger when he saw it.

'Er, Horak ain't it?' he fenced. 'What — '

'Papers,' Horak insisted, thrusting

out his left hand. 'C'mon, c'mon, don't look so dumb. Even cowpushers carry something — pay-slip, letters. I'll take anything that says you are what you say, namely a cowpoke on Smith's pay-roll. That's if Smith's the big geezer's name.'

The soldier hesitated awkwardly for too long. Abruptly Horak came clear, dim light winking on sixgun barrel, then came the ugly thud of the blow. The man, bleeding from the scalp, slumped to one knee, eyes rolling in their sockets.

'Cowboys never get cute with me,' Horak panted. 'Which means you sure ain't one.' The gun came down again and the bleeding trooper pitched forward into the straw, face down and out cold.

It took the gunman some time to locate the official Army personnel card hidden in the man's boot identifying him as Corporal Second Class, 15th Cavalry Regiment, Fort Comstock.

'Bluecoats!' he hissed, springing to his feet and delivering the unconscious figure a vicious kick. Then he whirled at the sound of a whistle and darted to the stable-doors to see the other three strangers making their way across the yard as Stark broke away from the fence corner with his hand covering his gun butt.

Kurt Horak's top lip curled as he whipped out his second pistol and stepped into the open. No fear in him, no caution or hesitation. In situations like this, he was at his best.

The house-guests froze when they became aware of him standing there with boots wide-planted and heavy legs locked firm at the knees, both manner and stance reflecting total assurance and menace. When you saw a man acting this cool, bucking danger, you just knew he had the goods.

'What?' the sergeant challenged, hands stealing to his waist. 'What's the guns about, mister? You gone loco or something?'

'Try the 'or something' — soldier boy!'

The trio paled as Horak drew papers from his breast pocket, flicked them and watched them flutter to the earth. The men saw what they were, and began backing up, reaching for their guns.

'What do you make of this, pard?' Horak called. 'Seems we got a bunch of goddamn true blue, guts and glory US Army soldier boys come to visit. Are we honoured or what?'

They thought he was foxing them, but when the sergeant snatched a look behind and sighted Stark's lanky figure standing there with his shadow stretched long across the yard and a big steel revolver in a gnarled hand, he knew they were in deep trouble.

'All right!' he shouted, raising his hand. ' You are right. We're Army on a special undercover assignment down here and you'd better be reminded it's a capital offence to interfere with a United States soldier in the field or — '

'Even if the lousy stinking bluebelly is caught sneaking into a man's town looking to get at men your dirty colonel keeps claiming are keeping the range wars burning?' Horak taunted. His voice grated like flint on flint. He was working himself up to something. 'Admit it, bluebelly. Your assignment is us — the Whiskeyville boys. Who were you after? Me? I'd have to be number one on your list . . . mainly because I *am* number one. What'd the colonel pep you up with? I'll tell you — it went like this: Get Horak at any cost. He's the one that gunned down Dunaway, then his own pards for siding with him. We can't take no more of Horak picking our people off thataway — so get down there to that rat-hole and nail his stinking hide to the wall and any more of those backshooting bastards you can.' He grinned like a wolf. 'Tell me it was different, big feller, go ahead.'

The sergeant's face was grey as the trio moved back in a tight little knot, facing not only Horak and Stark now but another three gunpackers, who, drawn by the uproar, were also holding guns on them as they narrowed the circle around them.

There was a taste of ashes in the mouth of Sergeant Flint now. He had been given command of an assignment planned by the colonel himself, the object of which was to escort his wife safely in to the fort by stealth and thus avoid the dangers prevalent in the county at an uncertain time. Now, not knowing even how it had come about, they'd been uncovered and were seemingly at the mercy of the very breed they'd been warned to avoid.

But Flint was a true soldier, and when he thought of the colonel's wife, he found the strength and resolution he needed.

He drew his revolver and stepped away from his men.

'This has nothing to do with Whiskeyville or you gunmen, Horak,' he stated flatly. 'You can take my word on that. But our job is vital, and I'm not about to allow anyone to interfere. So I'm ordering you to put away those guns and call off your men, and me and my party will be on our way quiet and peaceful, just as we planned.'

'Shuck your irons!'

Horak's voice rang harsh and flat across the wide yard. Clear and loud, it reached the ears of the onlookers watching from a safe distance and penetrated the doors and windows of the rooming-house. He tilted his revolvers a little and the sunlight winked on buffed steel. They were beautiful weapons with long octagonal barrels with the rammers underneath, blue and cold.

The cylinders were rounded at the ends like breasts; there was a sensual female curve to the down-sweep of thornwood stocks. Horak the killer was showing the guns and knowing the effect they must have, savouring the moment which for him was infinitely more exciting than anything he'd shared with the girl in his bed. 'I said drop, but you ain't dropped,' he said, his voice one rub above a whisper. The sergeant felt his blood had frozen in his veins. His surroundings seemed to have become a jumble of ragged shadows against a background of orange, gold and green. All he could see clearly now was Horak and his guns . . . the hot, winking gleam of those long-barrelled guns.

He knew what this soldier must do.

His gun arm jerked upwards and Horak gunned him down. Instantly the troopers began triggering. Joachim Stark absorbed a slab of bore-flame and the bullet tore through his spine, killing him where he stood.

A brief firestorm of angry gunfire and it was over, leaving three men lying dead, the big sergeant groaning on the ground clutching his thigh and Horak emotionlessly reloading as Whiskeyville's losers looked on agog. Whereas in almost any other town in the Territory such a grisly incident would evoke shock and horror, here it only seemed to engender wonder, curiosity and a sick kind of excitement.

Once again danger had come to their town and yet again Whiskeyville had proved that when it came to killing, nobody did it better.

6

THE HOSTAGE GAME

'Where'd they go?' croaked Benny the Gimp. 'Someone must've seen 'em come out of Deane's.'

'Mebbe we were all too busy watchin' Horak do his stuff on the chocolate soldiers,' speculated Johnny Silver, sunlight winking off his pistol foresight as he stood in the street, peering this way and that. 'Mule, you try the barn. Benny, check out the blacksmith's. The rest of you boys follow me. I'm bettin' they're hidin' in back of the store. C'mon, let's hustle!'

The sounds of voices faded and it grew quiet behind the closed doors of the saddler's shop where the three people within stood peering out through a scratch in the window glaze.

'Much obliged,' Clanton said to the saddler, a little man with bushy sideburns and pince-nez perched on the end of his nose. 'But why'd you take us in? This can only land you in trouble.'

'I cut Burk's hair once a month regular the past five years, son. He was a good man and a straight shooter. He often said you was the same.'

Trent nodded. Freemont was still helping him from beyond the grave.

'They'll still come hunting,' he predicted.

'So? You've got a breather, you and the lady. Better make the most of it and figure what you're going to do mighty quick. I'll go fix us a drink and keep watch out back.'

He ducked through an archway and Trent turned to the woman. He'd reacted instantly after taking one swift glance from the roomer at the violent scene erupting in the yard, taking her by the arm and getting out of there fast. They knew people had died but not who or how many. The town buzzed like a giant hive inhabited by killer bees. Trent was calm in a crisis as Freemont had always taught him to be. Somehow he was not surprised to see that Mrs Smith, though paler now and breathing hard from running, showed no sign of panic. Character was what they called it.

'You want to tell me what this is all about?' he invited. He made an incomplete gesture. 'I heard Horak accuse your men of being military — '

'They're soldiers escorting me home to Fort Comstock. I'm Colonel Blake's wife and . . . and I'm sorry to involve you, a perfect stranger, in this terrible mess.'

'I see.' He let a held breath run out of him slowly. He pulled his Colt and checked the loads. 'Better tell me the rest while we have time.'

It did not take long. Colonel Blake's plans for his wife sounded sensible enough to Clanton's ears, all factors considered. He reckoned the whole thing could easily have successfully had Horak only been out of town at the time. Trent nodded and deliberately took his time, twisting a smoke in steady hands. This had all the earmarks of as bad a scrape as he'd ever been in, but there was no way he would run or cave in simply because a dog-pack of gunpackers were on the howl. He was looking to figure a way through this without anyone else getting shot. Especially not her. He could well imagine the potential danger of Cara Blake's position should the hellers find out just who she was, and there had to be a strong chance they might.

And, he found himself thinking: especially not her.

'Then Horak's dead wrong if he's thinking your party arrived here looking to make a play against them?'

'Completely.' The woman drew closer, watching him lick the neat white cylinder into shape and place it between his lips. 'But tell me. Why did you do what you did just now? You could easily have been killed. You still could be. These people hate my husband because he represents the only law they have out here. It's not too late for you to leave by the back way. I would not think any the less of you if you did. They'll find me eventually whether you're with me or not, and if you stay you couldn't stand against so many, even if you wanted to.'

Smoke curled up before his face as he studied her with steady, level grey eyes. There was no simple answer to her question. He only knew he'd had to do it, would do it again and again if necessary.

Again he felt the sensation he'd experienced on first sighting her, something strange and disturbing.

He frowned in concentration. It was plain that before he would risk a showdown which he must surely lose, he had to exhaust all other possibilities, if indeed any existed.

'How can we convince Horak that what you say is so?' he asked, avoiding her question.

'I . . . I have Matthew's last letter advising me of his plans to have me escorted back to the post incognito.'

'That's a good start. Although that animal might only believe what he wants to.'

Cara made to reply but broke off as an unearthly shriek rose from further along the street. The scream hung in the air for a seemingly impossibly long time before eventually dying away in a series of agonized sobs.

The couple's eyes met and locked.

'Torturing the survivors to find out what they want to know,' he predicted. He saw her tremble and reached out and took her hand. 'We've got to face it. It's war out here. So, what else besides the letter?'

'I know Sergeant Flint has written authority to oversee the escort operation.'

'They'd have that now. I saw him go down but I don't think he took a mortal wound.'

'He's a very brave man.'

'And might need to be,' thought Trent, grimly. He returned to the window to peer out through the scratch. Johnny Silver, Dandy and Pedro were passing by on the opposite side of the street, throwing doors open and shouting, brandishing weapons. The gunners were trailed by a straggle of drunks and eager urchins, all plainly enjoying the 'fun'. It was a tragedy that Burk had spent his last years in a place like this, he found himself thinking. He'd deserved better. It would be an irony if both of them were to perish at the hands of the same man.

Further along by Gila's Bar he caught a fleeting glimpse of Horak's big figure as he strode from one side of the street to the other. The wind was whipping up dust devils and he thought he could smell the dead.

He swung back to her.

'I've got a plan. It's not much of a plan, but it might be the best on offer, considering we could well wind up dying on the spot if these trigger-happy vermin flush us out. Want to hear it?'

'You sound like Matthew when he's angry. But somehow you are more . . . forceful. Of course I want to hear, Trent. I feel we should be on first-name terms if we are not too sure if we'll live or die, don't you?'

'Cara,' he said, the word swallowed as a harsh shout wafted down the street.

'All right, Mrs Blake! We've scoured everything but the saddler's. You want to come out peaceable or do we shoot it into kindling wood? You better know I'm getting plenty sore!'

To Trent the killer's tone carried an impact that he couldn't ignore. They were trapped like rats.

'Well, they've got us now . . .'

He moved closer.

'I reckon we should give ourselves up and make a clean breast. Show him the letter, then do whatever we can to convince him that, whatever else he might think about the Army, your coming here had nothing to do with anything against them. You're cool and a good talker, and I have some standing with some of them because of Freemont. They're the positives. Of course the big negative is that we'd be dealing with a bunch of bloody-handed butchers headed up by a mad dog. What do you say?'

'What's the alternative?'

'Fort up here and shoot it out.'

'Ain't certain sure I like the sound of that all that much,' said the barber, reappearing with the drinks.

'Nor me,' Cara said, taking her glass and draining it at a gulp. She placed a hand on her breast and gasped, an achingly feminine gesture. 'I needed that — I think.' She gave Clanton a deep look, the kind of look, he imagined, front-line soldiers might dream of seeing before going into battle.

'I say we go out.'

He was aware of the dull thudding of his heartbeat as he drained the glass and set it aside. He was still cool enough, although conscious of the reality of their position. They could move out and walk into a hail of bullets. He'd never feared death before but had never felt less like dying. He sensed he knew why as he reached out to take Cara's hand. It was crazy, feeling this way at a time like this, but then maybe a little fraction of stolen time was all they had left.

What happened then was unlike anything he'd ever experienced, nor had ever expected to. As he drew her towards him, Cara kept coming until their bodies touched. Then she stretched up and kissed him full on the mouth. His arms went about her and they clung for a timeless, desperate moment until they heard the barber unlock his door.

'They's gettin' impatient, Freemont's kid.'

Moments later they emerged into the sunlight to see Kurt Horak standing there. They started their way, flanked by a dozen guns.

'Don't shoot!' the killer ordered, throwing up both arms, and there was no way any Whiskeyviller was about to disobey. Yet relieved as he was to find himself still breathing as the mob closed in, Clanton, studying Horak's iron features, couldn't believe the man was sparing them out of compassion. He had to have another reason, he figured.

And he did.

★   ★   ★

Gila's joint was doing big business. He had two girls working behind the bar and another woman — she would never be a girl again — and two porch-loafers working the crowded tables.

'It's an ill wind that doesn't blow somebody some good,' he confided in his cynical, one-eyed way to Whiskey George. 'This wind stirred up by the colonel's wife's sure certainly blown some welcome business trade our way today.'

Deadbeats and winos and down-at-heel derros who hadn't been able to raise the price of a drink in weeks, suddenly mustered sufficient resources to show up at the saloon. A man needed coin to fill a chair at Gila's; he wasn't running any kind of refuge for no-dollars layabouts, thank you.

The sergeant and the trooper occupied a wooden booth off to one side, the former ashen with pain with one leg stuck out stiffly before him, the young cavalryman unharmed in the shoot-out that had claimed two lives yet every bit as pale and drawn as the rugged noncom at his side.

The two men had no way of knowing what the purpose of Horak's assembly here might be. For all they knew this could prove to be a lynch mob court where they would be immediately tried and hanged by people who would not recognize the law if it woke them up in bed wearing a diaphanous nightdress. Two of their number had already been butchered like beeves, and they'd seen enough of Horak and his hangers-on already to realize that all the lurid stories they'd heard about this place were true — understated, if anything.

'I should've spoken out against the colonel's plan,' Flint lamented, taking a jolt of the whiskey provided by a sympathetic bar girl. 'I knew it'd be risky, coming by the badlands from Pearl. He should have either spared the men for a full escort up the east range, or told her not to come until things were looking safer. He'll be lucky to ever see her again now.'

'God, you don't think they would harm Mrs Blake, do you, Sarge? They wouldn't hurt a lady.'

'You've got a lot to learn, Junior. Your dog back on the post has got more breeding than these bastards. Take the blinkers off your eyes and have a look round. What do you think a woman's life would be to Joe Average from Whiskeyville? Ten cents? Less maybe. And don't forget they hate the colonel's guts. They'd top her just to square accounts with him and the Army for giving them a hard time since ever Blake took over. Hell, they'd do it even without a reason.'

Licking his lips, young Trooper Slattery was digesting this grim prediction when a buzz of anticipation swept through the barroom as Vinnie Gascoigne and Pedro entered. The hardcases had arrived bearing documents discovered stitched away in the soldier's effects.

But it quickly appeared that there was nothing incriminating to be found against the captives amongst the papers beyond substantiation of the prisoners' identity and the purpose behind their mission.

'Looks to me army intelligence is gettin' smarter and shiftier by the day, pards,' yelled Pedro, holding papers aloft. 'To me this crap looks like somethin' hatched up to fool us iffen they fell into our hands. What do you say?'

Gila's bar shook to a roar of approval. But it didn't mean a thing. The man in the street here had nothing against the Army, was simply craven enough to go along with just about anything the hard men amongst them suggested. Stand these surviving blue-coats up against Gila's cedar bar and shoot them down? If that's what Horak and the boys wanted — go right ahead.

Trent Clanton and Cara Blake heard the shouting as they crossed the street flanked by smirking outlaws. Hostage-taking was just another way of raising revenue here from time to time. But Whiskeyville had never had a catch like this. Suddenly it seemed they had shifted up a gear and crashed through into the big time. The gunmen could not hide their triumph; their prisoners did a far better job of concealing their apprehension.

'Why are they taking us to the saloon, do you imagine, Trent?'

'I'm hoping it's just to show you off to Mr and Mrs Whiskeyville.'

'You don't imagine they might put us — me, on trial of some kind, do you?'

'No, I reckon Horak just wants to gloat. Strikes me as a gloater — '

The rifle butt thudded against the side of his head and knocked him down. For a dizzy moment his vision turned crimson with rage as he tasted blood. Figures blurred in his sight then abruptly cleared as someone hooked a hand under his arm and hauled him erect. He stood swaying and spitting, the red film of rage gradually clearing from his eyes: *Never let the enemy see you're hurting, or know what you're really thinking, boy. That's another Burk Freemont tip on the noble art of survival in a cruel world, Trent.*

Freemont's wisdom had saved him before, did so now. He hung his head as though in submission as rifle-wielding Mule Hendry cussed him out, then handed him a warning. Keep his big mouth off Horak or suffer the consequences; did he understand?

'Sorry,' he made himself say. He raised his eyes to the hardcase. 'I've got nothing against Kurt, honest . . . '

'Even though he put Freemont in the bone orchard? Don't ask me to swallow

144

that, Clanton. You'd have Kurt's guts for garters if you could, which is why I wouldn't be in your boots thumbs down when we get to discussing your case.'

'Is that why you brought us here? Discussion?'

'Smart, huh? Better not play smart-mouth with Horak, cowboy.'

'Tell me, how come every man and his brother are talking up Horak as though he's number one?' Clanton challenged. 'I saw him around just yesterday and it seemed to be he couldn't find anyone to have a drink with him, yet today he's everybody's hero.'

'It was him who sniffed that army party out, then him what dealt with it,' Dandy reminded sourly. 'That's enough to make any man number one, for a day at least.'

Clanton was thoughtful as they approached Gila's crowded porch. Suddenly he was finding himself up against the whole town, whereas prior to Cara Blake's arrival he'd seemed to have achieved a high degree of acceptance. Yet it was easy enough to figure, he knew. His connection with Freemont had guaranteed his safety here until he'd linked up with Cara Blake, wife of the enemy.

And he let them all know exactly how he felt about this when, as Hendry went ahead to clear a way to the steps, he slipped a protective arm about the woman's shoulders as they mounted the porch and a bearded man with no teeth tried to block their way.

'Your husband hanged one of my good pards last year, bitch!' he accused. 'With any luck we'll git to hang you today.'

'Why don't you shut up?' Clanton said quietly.

The man lunged. He was full of whiskey and hate. Trent's blurring right elbow snapped upwards and smashed him savagely in nose and mouth. Blood splashed and the big man slumped to his knees as though his bones had turned to jelly.

Wide-eyed onlookers fell back and, holding Cara protectively again, he pushed on past to enter the saloon.

A sea of angry and accusing faces greeted the couple. Blood had spilled, liquor flowed, and emotions whipped up by talk of spy plots and secret army agendas were raging.

The Army had always been the enemy here. The law of the county didn't extend this deep into the heart of the Spearhead, so that the only real authority ever experienced here was that represented by Fort Comstock.

Yet Army and helltown had managed to coexist at a tolerable if uneasy level until recent times, when the ongoing feud between the Southern cattle barons had stretched Comstock's resources beyond their limits. Now with rumours of a pending truce between Moran and Quent and their illegal plans to mine the copper out at blood-soaked Kaw Hill, Army intervention was anticipated. Lawmakers of the Territory capital introduced the Cattle Amnesty Bill, which inevitably led to a mad scramble for cattle, the rise of widespread rustling and conflict between the town and the post.

The story they'd been fed today was that Colonel Blake had sent in a spy gang of soldiers in disguise, had even risked his own wife's life by including a woman in the bunch to give it more credibility. Horak had already invited them to consider a sobering question: could the arrival of the 'spies' be the precursor to an imminent Army attack?

From behind his bar, Gila watched and listened and rubbed his hands in secret glee. He enjoyed nothing better than upheaval, uncertainty, fear and anger, was never happier than when his clientèle was revealed as even more base, cowardly, vindictive and treacherous — as they were proving themselves today.

His only disappointment centered upon Freemont's kid and the woman. Both were so handsome and strong, yet he wanted to see them come apart and degrade themselves — which they showed no sign of doing as Dandy and Hendry attempted to force a way for them through the shouting and drunken mob.

Everyone whom Gila knew was sick, diseased, twisted or crippled either in body or spirit. By contrast, 'Freemont's kid' seemed normal, which surely made him the most freakish customer to walk though his batwings all year. And he could hardly wait to see how Horak would go about trimming him back to size. No sir. He would not walk so tall when that Kurt was through with him.

He wasn't the only one to feel that way, as Clanton was discovering. Vinnie Gascoigne cleared a space by the long bar. The gunman's eyes flared cold. 'We treated you right, Clanton, on account of Freemont. Seems to me he'd be spinnin' in his grave right now if he could see this, you turncoat bastard.'

'You've got me wrong,' Clanton said guardedly, standing at Cara's side. 'I'm not taking sides. Just didn't want to see Mrs Blake get hurt was all.'

'You reckon Burk would have give a damn about any snooty army-post piece?' the hardcase challenged. He snorted. 'He'd have been first to give her a feel or a smack in the head if she acted up — what do you say, sweetheart?'

With these words he reached out and squeezed Cara's breast. Trent let fly with a punch that belted the man up against the bar and set his eyes rolling in their sockets. Instantly Dandy shoved his gun against the back of Clanton's neck. He was cocking the hammer when a gunshot rocked the room and a chunk of plaster fell from the ceiling.

'Hold up, damnit!' roared Horak, emerging from a doorway in back to cleave through the mob towards the bar, the smoking gun still in his fist. 'Seems a man can't let you people out of his sight for a minute. Dandy, put that gun away, and someone toss some water over Vinnie.'

He halted before Trent with a thoughtful frown then slammed his gun against the side of his head, spilling him to the floor with a great clatter.

'OK,' he drawled, winking at Cara as he slipped his shooter away. 'This here court will now come to order.'

7

TOP DOG BARKING

The blow to the side of the head knocked the rustler sideways. A second trooper struck him across the back of the neck to send him spinning away against the third, who deliberately kneed him to the ground, gasping in pain.

'OK, OK,' panted the corporal, massaging his knuckles. 'So now we've introduced ourselves, Mr Crowe, let's not be shy any more, huh? Just tell us what we want to know and just mebbe we'll let up on you . . . you cow-thievin' little bastard. We know you ride for Hud Moran, so why not own to it?'

The rustler rose on one elbow, the guard room swimming in his vision. He'd been brought in by an Army detail following his apprehension on the East

Range north of Whiskeyville, driving a bunch of cows wearing a Combine brand. He was insisting on his innocence. Either he was touched by the sun or he seriously underestimated the determination of his interrogators.

'I'm a blacksmith by trade, and a man just asked me to mind them beeves while he — '

His words were chopped off as a boot drove into the small of his back. He tried to get up but the corporal kicked him again. He began to weep but this only seemed to inflame his captors. They were pummelling him heavily when the door opened and the colonel stood there, his face flushed with anger.

'Attention, damn you!' he yelled and three troopers snapped rigid. Fort Comstock's war with the rustlers and outlaws might well be intense, but whenever the top man was present you fought it by the rules. 'Take this man to the infirmary,' Blake ordered disgustedly. 'And consider yourselves on report. We'll see if ten days' guard duty might burn off some of your excessive zeal. Guards!'

Troopers came running and Blake strode from the room, sleeving sweat off his brow as he headed for administration.

He was genuinely angry with his men, for Colonel Matthew Blake did everything by the book. But he knew the real cause of his tension today had nothing to do with rustled beeves, badmen or unruly personnel.

Still no message from the south.

The last communication from Sergeant Flint had been wired from Pearl City almost sixty hours earlier. Had the party kept to schedule, the escort should have overnighted at Whiskeyville, then journeyed on to reach the telegraph station at Taloga many hours ago.

The colonel went directly down the corridor to Communications. Still nothing. His aide insisted it was too early to start worrying, but he was worrying like hell. As he glanced at the westering sun he realized that for the very first time since taking command at Comstock, he wasn't going to be able to wait until sundown to take his first drink.

Blake was anything but an alarmist, but he had had a sinking feeling ever since the very hour Flint's wire was officially classified as overdue, that something had gone wrong. And now with concern clawing at his guts, he discovered that not even whiskey could soothe him.

★   ★   ★

'It seems a pretty straightforward case to this court of justice,' smirked Horak from his perch seated atop Gila's bar. 'The way it figures out, the Army decides we're making out too good at the rustling game and all, so they send in an undercover squad to try and pick off our top guns. And who do you reckon they'd have been looking to nail first, huh?'

155

'Horak!' came the muted but clear-cut response, and he had to be content, even if he'd had to solicit the result. He'd long since given up any hope of achieving such spontaneous intangibles as friendship or admiration even from the men he was increasingly coming to dominate.

There were dark times when Horak suspected every man Jack of them hated his guts and wanted to see him dead. But today was different. Today's events had played his way. There'd been sudden danger, he'd quashed it in jig time, and now had them feeling they'd already won a telling victory against their nemesis, namely the Army of The United States. This should rate respect, at least. And grudging or not, he was determined to get it.

Continuing on with his parody of a real court of law, he was working them up against the 'accused' and their 'accomplice', the man he liked to call 'Freemont's boy'. Gila, the tireless observer of the sick and murderous, watched almost admiringly from the fortress of his bar and thought: 'He's finally made it to where he's always wanted to be — the cold-blooded varmint. Who'd ever have thought it. At last some of these losers seem to think he's something.' He sneered. 'But it can't last. Once a bloody-handed scum-dog always, Horak . . . '

The smirk vanished to be replaced by a big empty grin when Horak happened to glance his way. Next thing, Gila was joining with the others to put his hands together to applaud what the big killer was proposing as about the only suitable punishment for those involved in the conspiracy against him here. Death.

Life was dirt cheap in Whiskeyville and the noisy response indicated that nobody really considered this fate in any way excessive for enemies who plotted against them. Shouts of 'Hang them! Shoot them!' and 'Give us the skirt first!' rocked the rafters, and Horak urged them on, pumping his fist in the air while the four captives looked on stonily from the sidelines.

Despite the fact that Burk Freemont's regular letters had made it clear just what kind of town Whiskeyville might be, Trent Clanton still found it hard to believe what he was witnessing here. He'd attempted to offer a defence earlier, but brutal gunbutts had silenced him. He tried again now, but was chanted down. The mob had seen blood and wanted more. What he had to say didn't matter one damn.

He wanted to believe that, had Burk been alive today, he would behave far better than his friends and henchmen arrayed before him now.

Gila clapped hands in eager expectation when it grew obvious that the worked-up mob was on the verge of getting out of hand, the heady combination of free-flowing liquor and Horak's rhetoric whipping them up.

Then, unpredictable as always, the master of ceremonies suddenly crashed another shot into the roof and looked ready to put the next round into the crowd if they didn't hush quick smart. He was glowering and sober again as he thrust his gun away.

'You poor boneheads,' he sneered. 'Fifty of you sharing the same brain!'

They stared, not understanding. Why was he mocking them now?

'What do you mean?' growled Vinnie Gascoigne, a man close to Horak in stature and ability, touchy too.

'Mebbe I'm referring to your last job, Vinny,' Horak retorted, jumping down from his perch 'Remember?'

Gascoigne's scowl cut deep. The job referred to had been to lay the groundwork for the all-important Moran-Quent peace conference right here in Whiskeyville.

What connection that might have with what was going on here now none could figure.

'OK, OK,' Horak said impatiently, eager to reveal his cleverness. 'If you can't see it I'll spell it for you. All of you.'

He halted and folded heavy arms, eyes cutting from face to face as he went on.

'Now I don't know how many of you have got wind of something mighty important I've been lining up here this week, but you can take my word for it that it's on and it's big. So big in fact that if the Army got wind of it and guessed what we were really up to, Blake would haul his troops out of the Injun country and come looking for us at the gallop — you can take that as gospel truth. All right. We're being double careful, yet a thing like that could happen.' He paused for emphasis. 'But it won't happen now. Know why? Come on. Last chance for some big brain to guess what I'm leading up to.'

Trent Clanton glanced sideways at Cara Blake to find her staring directly up at him, wide-eyed yet outwardly calm. She knew, he realized. But they appeared to be the only ones who did.

'It won't freaking happen because suddenly I'm holding that dung-eating

Frontier Army right here in the palm of my hand, goddamnit!'

Horak strode triumphantly across to reach Cara's side before swinging about to face the mob again.

'Blake's wife . . . hostage . . . get it? I'll order that lousy bluecoat colonel to get down on his lousy stinking knees and come crawling all the way across the goddamn desert to agree to anything we damn well want — or we'll send him her head in a gunny sack? You catching on now?'

There was a brief moment for the sheer scope of this to sink in. Then genuine cheering and acclaim suddenly erupted on all sides of the grim-faced prisoners, telling the four that Whiskeyville finally understood. And Trent saw Cara drop her dark head, her hands clenching in her lap.

His expression was blank as he looked up but it was tough to keep it that way. Inside he was raging, but not necessarily at the far-reaching ramifications of what had just been revealed.

161

If he'd entertained any doubts about his feelings towards this woman who had entered his life so dramatically, they were brushed aside in that moment when he realized he was only concerned about her.

Then he shook his head and forced himself to concentrate on the full scope of Horak's threat. If scumtown Whiskeyville could force Blake into submission and so render the Army impotent, even for a period, then the lawless would take over to dominate this benighted country as never before.

A man could only guess just how long it would take to bury the dead if these outlaws broke out of their desert cage with someone like Horak leading them.

A grinning pygmy with live things in his hair came prancing up to the prisoners, bugged his eyes then reached for Cara. Clanton's right boot lashed out and sunk into the bum's groin. The pygmy fell in a howling heap and a sour, swag-bellied man swinging a bar stool came charging in.

The crash of Horak's sixgun was deafening in the confined space, and the stool-wielder collapsed, clutching a bloodied leg.

'We ain't gonna damage our trade goods until we get what we want!' he stated, gunsmoke writhing his body. Then he turned and slapped the bartop and hollered for drinks all round. Immediately the excitement rose again, serving-girls quickly began pouring shots and evil-faced men cheered and stomped until the rafters trembled and spiders, dead and alive, began dropping from the gloom, adding to the wild mood.

It was so long since Whiskeyville had had anything to celebrate that nobody was about to pass up the opportunity. There was no telling how long the good times might last.

Threading his way through the revellers, Horak approached Cara and chucked her under the chin.

'Cheer up, lady, you'll be fine. Once

your old man has served up this county to us on a platter he can have you back. I'm not a mean man. Just on account you happen to be with that bluecoat bastard who's put some of my best pals in jail or in the ground, doesn't mean I can't be generous . . .'

He paused as though taken by a new thought.

'Hey — but mebbe right now you could be wondering if your colonel might be sitting back wondering if you're worth it or not.' His eyes twinkled maliciously. 'Hey, that thought never crossed my mind. I mean, you being kinda juicy, and your long-nosed colonel being such a gent of the old school, or so they claim, I figured it'd be natural he wouldn't be able to wait to make himself a hero by coming to collect you, post-haste. But what . . . what if after he knows we've got you he simply don't give a damn? Now there's a black thought and no mistake.'

'Why don't you leave her alone?' Clanton growled. 'You're holding top cards. What more do you want?'

'What I want, Freemont's pal, is to decide what's to be done with you, the geezer who turned against his own, like Judas.'

'I'm not one of you.'

'We've treated you like one.' Horak gestured. ''Most everyone here wanted you given a fair run on account most everyone liked Freemont. I sure as hell never did, but most did. So we all treated you fine, cowhand. Yet for our pains you kick us in the teeth. What do you reckon I should do if you were in my boots?'

'Get rid of him, Kurt,' advised the fuzzy-headed freak Clanton had floored earlier. 'I'll handle it if you want.'

'Hey, hold up there a minute!' called a voice from the bar, and all turned to see Gila leaning forward on bony elbows, solitary eye bright with malice. 'It seems to me you'd be missing out on an opportunity for some real fun if you was to top that cowboy, Horak.'

He enumerated on his fingers.

'Number one, we get to dragging the colonel down here to rub his long nose in it. Two, we get to sit back and watch him squirm as he tries to decide whether he thinks more of his woman than he does of his dirty profession. Then three — the best part of the entertainment and the bonus — we can watch what breaks when Blake finds out his wife's got the hot yearnings for someone else.'

'What?' Horak seemed puzzled. 'What are you talking about, you one-eyed freak?'

Gila triumphantly indicated the couple seated together on the hard-wood bench. 'Romeo and Juliet. I saw it the moment they came in, and you know I'm never wrong about these things. Colonel Blake's immaculate wife has only got eyes for Freemont's kid, and it wouldn't surprise me one lick if he doesn't feel the same way about her. Now, does this add the straight shot after the beer, or doesn't it?'

Horak stepped back a pace to stare

sharply from Clanton to Cara. The couple returned his look expressionlessly, yet he still slapped his thigh with sudden boisterous delight.

'B'God, I declare you just might have something, you miserable fraud.' He swung to face his henchmen. 'And who knows? All this could work our way if we handle it right . . . better even than we'd figured . . . '

He paused thoughtfully before snapping his fingers. He gestured briskly.

'OK, this is how we'll go about it. We'll hold this prize pair at the roomer along with the other two . . . we could just need all the hostages we can rustle up before we're through with the colonel. And Vinnie, you come with me. I'll write up the message and you can hotfoot it to the telegraph at Taloga and get it off to Blake. So, what are you waiting for? Let's hustle.'

Outside the sun was sliding below the rim of the desert. It was that hour when the first bats appear and the coyotes yip from the lonely hills. The time when the water-carter sets off for the day's last journey to the river, and even the plank shacks, mud huts and creek-side lean-tos are invested with something like beauty . . . as prisoners and escort moved across the rutted street.

In the dust-blue dusk of Whiskeyville, the windows seemed to stare out blindly. The careworn stairways and the wind-scoured walls of a town too ugly to live all appeared suddenly and improbably lovely to the eyes of four people who sensed they might be seeing them for the last time.

Horak said they would live. But who would believe a man like that if he said the sun would rise tomorrow?

'Well, hush, O hush,
Somebody's callin' me.
Well, hush, O hush,
Somebody's callin' me home.'

The sounds of the softly sung spiritual drifting across the empty parade-ground seemed to stir the curtains of the colonel's spartan quarters and penetrate the room where he sat on a camp-stool packing away the last of his equipment into his satchel.

He paused to listen. The Negro soldiers' evensong mostly made him feel good but tonight's words and music seemed painfully apt and filled him with foreboding. Somebody calling all right. Ruin, disaster, maybe even death itself; that was what just might be calling.

He could take it had it been the case that Fate might only be calling for him. But this was not the case. His wife was in desperate peril, and making the situation immeasurably worse was the raw and ugly fact that it was he who'd put her there. And now they'd sent for him and he must go.

Somebody calling?

What else could it be calling for Colonel Blake but the voice of disaster and ruin?

He shook himself as he stood erect. Enough of that! he chided himself. He was a man with a lifetime of self-discipline behind him, he reminded himself. He searched for this strength and discovered he still had it, despite finding himself in the toughest situation of his life.

He took up his valise and quit the room, striding through the quarters which he'd had redecorated in anticipation of his wife's return, polished boots clicking on bare boards as he went out.

He found young Lieutenant Roades waiting for him directly outside. The man's face fell when he saw the valise.

'So . . . so you intend going through with this, Colonel?'

'There is no alternative.'

'But you can't just abandon your command, sir. You'll be throwing away your career, apart from exposing the Company to danger without your leadership. Please, sir, just a minute . . .'

But Blake was already striding away, back rigid, knuckles showing white so tightly did he grip the handle of his valise. Ever since the arrival of the wire from Taloga he'd known what he would do; what he must do. It had taken all day to complete his preparations for departure; he would never leave the post unprepared no matter what his outspoken lieutenant might think. Fort Comstock would carry on, but if his action was to cost him his career then so be it. He was playing for bigger stakes than that.

A short time later the stockade gates swung open and a single rider emerged. The parapet guards saluted and the gates were slowly hauled shut again. The colonel rode south, heading into the desert.

8

FIRST KILL

Momma Deane dabbed at her eyes.

'Ain't it a crying shame! And ain't they just the handsomest couple you ever did see? I swear I don't know what's coming over this town when plain folks like us are supposed to act as jailers for beautiful people like them. Tell me what's happening to Whiskeyville, Papa, you always act as though you know everything.'

This was not a compliment, as the host of Deane's Room and Board was well aware.

'If I did know I doubt I'd be telling you, woman,' silver-haired Papa Deane replied glumly. 'The way you talk, you'd likely tell the whole world, and next thing I know someone with a gun would come knocking on my door.'

'You're a fearful man, Papa Deane, that's your trouble.'

'Mebbe. But I'm alive, ain't I? Which is more than you can say for the last man to speak out against Horak, or for these four unlucky ones who ain't likely to be alive much longer if you ask me.'

Momma Deane broke down at this point, retiring to their quarters with a double rum and sarsaparilla. Year in, year out, she catered to all the losers and nobodies who could afford the modest tariff at the roomer, yet the moment some people of real class showed she found herself obliged to evict her regulars and accept the role of jailer for the prisoners until Horak decided what was to become of them.

The Deanes hated Horak, but feared him even more. Nobody in Whiskeyville was forgetting the Freemont lesson. If Horak could get away with killing the town's favourite son, who was safe from him here?

Trent Clanton certainly considered himself to be lucky to be still breathing as he sat smoking by the parlour window staring out at the moonlight. From the outset he'd figured Horak as a mad dog with a gun. He'd challenged the man by trying to help Cara, yet was still alive.

Good luck or good connections?

His money was on the latter. The way he saw it, Horak was riding high yet was stretching himself at the moment and still attracted plenty of resentment over Freemont's death. He could kill Clanton, sure. But that might inflame sentiment against him further. In any case, the man probably didn't regard 'Freemont's friend' as significant enough to waste a bullet on right now.

After all, what harm could a cowboy from Kansas cause a man like that in Whiskeyville, his lethal hometown?

Clanton looked calm enough, and the slums had sure taught him how to survive simply by keeping low when the danger-level was high.

Even so he was aware that right now he still wanted to buckle on a gun,

174

throw Cara astride a fast horse, then blast his way to freedom tonight just as Freemont would have done in his shoes.

He hoped he wouldn't. The truth was that, in this moon-drifting hour, Trent Clanton was being torn in different directions. He craved the release of violent action, yet was held back by concern for others. His will held him passive while his very nature demanded he act. He was acutely conscious, during that endless hour, that he was two men, the responsible ramrod and the man whom his surrogate father had taught the craft of the gun.

There was no presentiment of immediate crisis as he stubbed out his cigarette, darted a last glance around his improvised prison, then went down the silent hallway to his room.

He swung the door open and immediately sensed a presence. His mouth went dry. He was half-expecting Horak might order him finished off sooner or later, feared this could be it.

A gunblast in the dark — oblivion. Was this how it was to be?

'Who's there?' he demanded.

'It's all right, Trent, it's me.'

He closed the door and moved to the bed, now able to make out her seated figure. He sat beside her and felt for her hands. She was cold and trembling.

'I had to come, Trent. I'm so afraid, so sickened by what is happening. I . . . I just couldn't bear to be alone.'

'It's OK, Cara . . . it's fine.'

He'd never meant anything more in his life. From the moment they'd met he'd known this was not just an attractive woman but the woman. The one he'd been searching for and never found — somebody dramatically different from all the girls he'd known, the ones who'd never meant more than a night's fun or a buggy-ride in the country.

Suddenly they were embracing and he realized that from the very beginning he'd wanted to take her in his arms as he was doing now, to kiss her this way without being plagued by guilt or conscience. To acknowledge that, from the first moment he'd set eyes on the colonel's wife, he'd suspected that the seemingly impossible had happened to him in his hard-driven, lonesome life. That the barriers his solitary life had erected about him had at last come crashing down. There was no telling how long they were together in the velvet darkness as desert stars followed their eternal course across an innocent night sky and ugly men toting guns prowled the streets close by outside. For here, for a brief time at least, fear and death were banished from a beat-up roomer in a night of peril in the heart of the Territory's ugliest town.

'I love you, Trent,' she cried. 'I can't believe it, I don't wish it, but I do.'

'I've waited all my life for this.'

'We'll never be apart.'

'Never — I swear.'

She laughed softly and kissed him. Then cried. And fought him off and urged him on. Joyfully accepting everything he had to give and holding back nothing, all demons driven off, these sole occupants of the entire universe finally collapsing against one another, arms entwined, breathing and touching until Clanton felt himself smile as he realized she had slipped off to sleep like a tired child with tears on her cheeks. He knew he must come down to earth, but not yet.

* * *

Horak sat up with a start. Gila's was deserted. Two dim lamps still burned and a candle guttered in its metal sconce above his table.

Alone again.

He lunged to his feet and kicked his chair over with a crash, spitting curses that nobody heard.

There was seldom a clear reason behind some of the killer's worst rages. He could make the transition from frivolity to murderousness and back again without any cause that anyone might be aware of. He did not need insults, challenges or dangers to trigger him off. A notion, an idea, a thin suspicion or an irrational hunch could do it just as easily. As a result, even though this man had somehow clawed his way to top of the heap here in recent weeks, he still could not boast a single genuine friend, or one woman who didn't fear him more than they might have otherwise cared for him.

His hat was askew and he was hitching at his gunbelt as he made his stiff-legged way across to the bar. Rows of silent bottles glinted in the feeble lamplight and the gunman felt a tight lump in his throat. He was always alone. This was nothing new, but tonight he thought it might have been different. For yesterday had seen him stage a major coup that might well result in big money and opportunities coming to Whiskeyville. He'd snared the colonel's wife and parlayed that into a scam which, if successful, could cancel out the threat of the Army and really put this town on the map.

He could see it now.

Without Comstock to worry them, he would be free to bring on the peace talks between Moran and Quent and stitch up the mining deal which he knew both cattlemen were eager for. From this would flow mining, land, power — and Kurt Horak would be king of the heap!

He knew Whiskeyville realized this was the way things were heading, and who was responsible. But how did his success translate?

Yesterday he'd been top dog. Tonight there wasn't even one whore or a solitary boozehound to share the night. Ungrateful bastards!

His mood was worsening dangerously as he stomped stiffly from Gila's to cross the porch and stand in the street with his face to the gritty wind blowing in off a hundred miles of wasteland.

Whiskeyville lay shrouded in darkness but for dim lights showing at

Deane's and the hotel, brighter ones along at the Double Hitch.

He bit his lower lip as he strode down to the town's second saloon. Drunken voices raised in song reached him as he approached, and he shouldered his way in to the sight of hunched nightowls sprawled untidily around a big circular table littered with bottles, ashtrays and discarded poker-chips, all very plainly both feeling no pain and enjoying one another's company.

Each one here had been at Gila's earlier, cheering him to the echo. Yet in the end all had quit the place to come down here — away from him.

Afterwards, none of the hardcases was too clear exactly what happened beyond the fact that Horak came in and immediately began snarling and raving, kicking the furniture about, hurling insults, until Mule Hendry made to rise from his chair. Maybe it could have appeared to Horak as if Hendry was reaching for his Colt; nobody could be sure afterwards. What was incontestable was that Horak jerked out both Colts with a curse and opened up at twenty-feet range to blow the big man backwards over his chair. Hendry hit the floor hard but still managed to claw his Peacemaker out and up despite the fact he was dying. He triggered once before a slug split his forehead and he was dead before his head struck the boards.

'Bastards!'

Horak's voice dimly reached ears half-deafened by the gunfire. He had killed a man and looked ready to kill more; why, nobody could begin to guess. But every shaking hardcase kept his hands on the table in clear view and his lips buttoned tight until the madness slowly left the gunman's eyes. Abruptly Horak holstered his weapons and strode out, slamming empty hands against the batwings so violently that one door broke off its hinges and clattered noisily to the porchboards.

In the sucked-out silence that followed all Whiskeyville could be heard coming awake.

'What?' gasped Johnny Silver. 'Boy shot the Mule, you say? You gotta be joking.'

'Straight A, God's truth.' Dancer Dandy's gaunt features were still bloodless and pinched-looking in the pallid starlight of the roomer's side yard.

'Drilled him cold, straight out-of-the-box — just like that. Where's the others?'

Watching the scene from behind the drapes of the supper room, Trent Clanton watched the pair hurry away across the yard towards the alley end of the building. He noted that Silver had his nickel-plated gun in hand and kept swivelling his head around as though half-expecting danger to appear at any moment. And who wouldn't?

It took mere moments to return to his room. Yet that proved time enough to reach what was probably the most momentous decision of his life.

This was breakout time.

As though anticipating his intentions,

Cara was up and dressed, was just drawing her hair back into a ribbon at her neck as he entered the room.

'Darling,' she whispered, 'what is it?'

He told her Horak had apparently just slain one of his own, and now the whole town was in uproar.

His summation of the situation was simple; they might never get another chance like this.

'What chance is that, Trent? What are you saying?'

He seized her by the shoulders, streetlight limning his profile, fingers digging into soft flesh.

'That man is kill-crazy, Cara. I guessed it at the start, now he's just proved it. I figured we might be able to handle him, con or flatter him into keeping us alive long enough for us to figure a way to escape. But you can't deal with a crazy, can't take the risk. I'm not about to set around here until he decides to finish me, or turn you over to his scum for sport.' He clamped his jaws and thrust her towards the door. 'We're running.'

He expected resistance. Instead she raised herself on tiptoe and kissed his mouth.

'If we're together then nothing can harm us,' she said. 'Which way?'

It was hard to believe they could have come this far, this fast. Amazing but as real as anything he'd ever encountered. When Loner Clanton had finally fallen he'd fallen all the way. The colonel's wife too. Her eyes told him so; her words affirmed it.

Seizing her hand he led the way quickly along the gloomy passageway. There were only two entry doors to the roomer, both in the enclosed sleepout. He didn't spare a glance for the padlocked door of the soldiers' rooms. Flint and Slattery were considered dangerous, and were paying the price. He knew how lucky he was that their captors didn't regard him in the same light. Yet dangerous was exactly how he felt, and was, as they reached the sleepout and hustled along it towards the northern door at the yard end. No holding back now. He was back in Laredo, the world was against him, but he would survive.

He must, for her.

The door was latched on the outside but he was able to ease up a small window. He reached through and undid it. They froze as someone ran by, stood staring breathlessly at one another in the gloom until the steps faded. Trent glanced out. The yard stood empty. The murmur of voices told him people were gathering down by the alleyway. With lights going on and men calling across open spaces to one another in the confusion, Whiskeyville felt like the scariest place in the Territory at the moment.

'Wait here,' he panted and was gone before she could reply.

He felt exposed darting across the yard, gasped in relief as the stables loomed and he darted inside.

The moment he sighted the shadowy figure of a man reaching up to take a rifle down from the wall, unaware of his

186

cat-footed entry, the iron feeling inside told him that on this night he'd completed the full transition from simple range boss to whatever it was Freemont had stubbornly tried to mould him into.

He was at last a man who knew he could kill.

He had a powerful sensation of Burk at his side, reminding him how it should be done: fast, silent and final.

The stableman never knew what hit him. He went down in a heap and Clanton's hands blurred as he tore off his double gunrig, buckled it around his flat middle and grabbed up the Winchester.

Now he was armed and dangerous.

The raised voices outside concealed the noise he made saddling the horses. Sweat leaked from every pore in the chilly night. *Keep calm no matter what . . . panic's killed more good men than bullets . . .*

'Sure, whatever you say, Burk . . . ' he whispered.

Now came the desperate part. There was a rear door to the stables. He eased the animals outside without incident and held them tight in the shadow of the wall. But fifty feet of open yard lay between himself and the roomer, where he could barely make out Cara's dim shape in the darkness of the doorway. He stiffened at the sound of approaching steps. A foul-cursing Dandy went lunging by some distance away, was quickly gone.

Trent craned his neck around the corner to snatch a glance to his right. The yard now stood empty!

He beckoned vigorously and Cara came running, feet flying over the hard-packed dirt of the yard. They made it into their saddles and were swinging the horses for the gate when the shout reached them.

'What the hell . . . ? Who's that? Hold up!'

He hipped around in his saddle to see the flashy figure of Dandy coming around the south-east corner of the roomer.

Jerking to a stop on sighting them, the Dancer cleared his right-hand gun. But Clanton's gunsights were already locking in on the flashy figure, finger tightening on trigger. The revolver bucked in violent recoil and a plume of purple-shot smoke streaked across the yard and thudded home with a sound like an axe biting wet wood.

It was the ugliest sound Clanton had ever heard. The outlaw straightened from his crouch, his expression blank. Blood squirted through locked teeth. Falling backwards, he dragged a stool down with him . . . a final gesture from clawing fingers . . .

Everything happened at once.

A wild-eyed man rushed from a lopsided building and began firing at nothing.

Immediately a rifle answered from above and the man appeared to trip over his own feet and fell face downward in the street.

In moments the whole town was erupting, riding a lightning bolt of fear and uncertainty. But there was one man who knew exactly what he was doing and just where he was going. But not alone. Cara was swinging up at his side, and the gate stood wide.

'Go!' he roared at the top of his lungs as a bullet smacked close. 'Hup!'

They burst from the yard to go hammering along the back street side by side, the drumbeat of the horse's hoofs echoing back at them from barn, hotel and livery, drowning out the screams of fear and outrage behind.

They covered a block and were streaking for the surrounding gloom as a single rifle opened up from someplace, bullets ripping long furrows of dust. But the light was poor, the rifleman too eager, and it just could be someone was watching over them.

The night swallowed them whole.

9

A FOOL ON HORSEBACK

The night was done and early-morning light lay scattered about like broken glass as sleepless Whiskeyville emerged to face the day.

Horak sat quietly cleaning his guns.

It was unnerving for those watching from across the street to see him seated so relaxed there on the saloon porch. Yet every watcher had the uneasy feeling it was just a pose. That behind the blank face was a volcano that could erupt at any moment, and anyone standing too close had best watch out.

Not so.

The outlaw's calm was genuine. He knew he had lost control when he gunned down Mule Hendry, thereby undermining his hard-won support. He'd almost wrecked everything on the very day he hoped to secure the full support of his cattlemen associates, after neutralizing Fort Comstock through its commandant, whom he expected to show up through the dunes and tumbleweeds any time now.

He'd wired Blake from Taloga to come alone if he ever wanted to see his wife alive again, and Blake had wired back that he was on his way.

Moran and Quent were due to arrive any moment to sit down, bury old differences and unite at last to take up the long-neglected challenge of the coppermine in the Funerals, each rich man's dream.

Three years earlier, a ragged-ass prospector named Billy Kipp had lucked upon the seam at Kaw Hill, shortly before Horak had first showed his face in Whiskeyville. Kipp had his find assayed and it proved to be the real thing. But all the miner had ever gotten out of his shallow hole was barely enough metal to keep him from starving to death.

The reason? The Funerals were too far from town to be safe for a mining operation, the Indians too dominant up there, except for a major operation. But the main problem had always been Moran and Quent. Each rancher itched to take over and develop Kaw Hill, but their bitter rivalry made it impossible for either one to start up the mine without attracting the intervention of the other.

That situation had prevailed well before Whiskeyville eventually threw up a man in Horak who proved smart enough to envision just how these prevailing conditions could change, how he might pull out all together — but for one thing.

The Army, the desert outlaw's number one enemy.

Trouble and bloodshed were an everyday factor of life, and Comstock lacked the manpower to maintain an ongoing presence here. But whenever major trouble erupted Blake would dispatch cavalry to settle things down, and this proved an ongoing deterrent.

Nothing major, either good or bad, could happen in the desert without the Army exerting its authority, sooner or later.

It had been a long wait for Horak, eager to develop the Kaw Hill copper of the mine, while aware that any serious attempt to do so would either trigger off the violent rivalry between the cattle barons, or bring the bluecoats back.

So he'd sat on his dream until the day the colonel's wife dropped into his lap like a ripe plum. The moment he realized his stroke of luck Horak was in the saddle and heading south to visit two hate-ridden old cattlemen with his proposal.

He made it sound almost simple.

The Combine and Big Six must first bury the hatchet; that was basic. Then Horak would simply utilize his hostage as a weapon to ensure Blake kept his troopers out of the desert while the digging got started up on Kaw Hill. Deeply impressed by developments,

Moran and Quent had immediately recognized the possibilities and the agreement was cemented, greed winning out over personal enmity with scarce a moment's hesitation.

Horak blew a speck from a sixgun hammer and smiled. Regardless of a slip-up, he was still *numero uno* in this hell-hole, and nobody could threaten him but himself. Only Horak could bring Horak down, and he made a vow not to do that again. From here on he would respond to changing situations exactly the way only a true leader should.

He stared across the bleak sandhills and crags. No sign of the dozen or so riders he'd dispatched to run down Clanton and his hostage. But he was totally confident they would succeed. His hellers were desert-wise; what chance would a hick cowboy and a woman have of escaping them here on their own turf?

His jaw muscles worked and his scowl cut deep.

'Freemont's kid' would die the

moment they hauled him back. He had completely misread Clanton, and now that hick had set everything he'd planned at risk. He refused to consider the one-in-a-thousand possibility of the runaways meeting up with Blake out there, in which case his entire master plan would come to zero. If he should fail again he knew he'd be in trouble here. He'd survived one major blunder but doubted his enemies would forgive him a second.

He was dreamily stroking the long octagonal barrel of a sixgun with a soft cloth when batwings creaked behind him and Gila appeared, toting a mug of coffee.

'Set it down and get lost, One-Eye.'

'Whatever you say, Kurt.'

'That's right — whatever I say.'

After a moment he raised his eyes to gaze across at the others, Tyrell, O'Hare, Gascoigne, Johnny Silver, Pedro and their hangers-on. One by one all but Silver dropped their eyes, which told Horak there would be no rebellion now.

No plans to shoot him in the back

and maybe then go on to hold a big wake for Silver's pard, Mule Hendry.

He was still the man.

His gaze drifted desertwards where there showed a distant flicker of movement, barely visible. Beneath a low-hanging dust cloud out there, something or somebody was travelling the buffalo trail from the south-east.

Horsemen, he soon realized.

Horak rose and holstered. He gestured curtly and men ran to their horses to go spurring out to meet the party. It was just a precaution, he mused. He expected it to be Moran and Quent, and so it proved to be.

One hour after that event, on the biggest day in the life of an outlaw town, a grim-faced Colonel Matthew Blake rode in alone out of the heat haze and entered the dusty street on a played-out Army horse.

Horak had hooked his fish. Now all he must do was locate the vital bait.

*   *   *

Amber was changing the dressing on Clanton's leg wound. It was no more than a crease, and although both Cara and the Council Creek girl were fussing over him, he knew it wasn't serious. Knew he could ride a hundred miles straight and hard, if pushed. But for the present he appeared ready to go along with the opinion of both women that he should rest.

It was close to sundown, yet the escapers were still here where there was a very real danger of discovery. It stood to reason that Horak would have men out scouring the desert for Cara, for she was the outlaw's ace-in-the-hole in the power game he was playing against her husband. Surely only a fool would tarry here when there was no real need. Or was Trent Clanton's reason for delay more complicated than that?

He rose from the stool and limped between weather-beaten shacks with the Winchester over his shoulder and sixshooters sagging from cutaway holsters, outlaw style. To ragged villagers and brown-skinned children he might well have been a Whiskeyville rider, and it was a sobering thought for him to reflect that over the past twenty-four hours he often felt he was acting less like a ramrod and more like the lawless breed he'd always despised.

He wondered if Freemont would have been impressed to see how he had changed. He knew *he* was not.

All day he'd sat under a tree on the rise, watching and waiting; watching for trouble and waiting to make a decision to ride on. This decision could come from either of them, he knew. If Cara said go, he knew he would go, and vice versa. But neither had suggested quitting since reaching Council Creek. Both understood the reason. The shadow of Whiskeyville lay across them still. There were innocent people back there living in fear of their lives with Horak now in sole command.

In addition was their understanding that Horak had dispatched a rider up to the telegraph at Taloga to wire Colonel

Blake at Fort Comstock, advising of his wife's capture. They feared this might impel Blake to come searching for Cara, either alone or in force.

All this was understood.

It troubled Trent to know that by quitting the region altogether he might be leaving Whiskeyville and maybe the entire Spearhead at serious risk.

He frowned and shook his head. Nothing much holding them here, he tried to convince himself. Then his expression changed as he scanned the blasted landscape for the hundredth time. *Nothing here, ramrod,* an inner voice seemed to whisper. *Nothing but wishy-washy things of no concern like decency, human lives at risk . . . conscience.*

Iron intangibles.

When Cara joined him the sun was low, the fierce heat already receding. She sat at his feet and the silence between them was complete despite their situation. Every passing hour reinforced the knowledge that the

200

magical thing they'd found together was real and total. She had never loved her husband any more than Clanton had ever loved another — so they had confided to one another. He believed her when she said that her marriage had been a suitable and sensible union for both her and Blake at the outset, but had been crumbling long before she came to Whiskeyville.

For Clanton it had been much simpler. Long before Whiskeyville, he'd virtually come to accept the fact that he was a man destined to know love yet never to fall in love.

Ever since Laredo he believed it had been given to him that he live his life alone but for the occasional friendship or brief liaison. A solitary man whose capacity to give or attract love had been ground out of him by the brutality and murderous desperation of his early life. Other men like him had formed friendships by the score; he'd only ever known one. He liked women but had never loved one, not even for a moment.

Certainly not the way he did here.

He frowned as he looked over his shoulder, troubling thoughts of Whiskeyville intruding again. What if that hell-hole was to grow strong and rich and come to dominate the entire Spearhead, Clanton? But even if that was on the cards, what could they do? What could anyone? He'd heard Horak boast of great plans coming to fruition after 'spiking the guns of the Army'. And who could tell? By this time he might even have succeeded in doing both.

So what was holding them here?

The couple stiffened when the dark shape of a horseman appeared suddenly out along the twist of the low-running creek back to the south, the direction they'd come from. Instantly Clanton hefted and cocked his rifle. He searched for more riders but there appeared to be just the one, and he was soon able to identify flash Johnny Silver, former partner of the late Mule Hendry.

'Could be a trick of some kind.

Mebbe Horak sent Silver in to get the lie of the land,' he speculated. 'Get back down and alert the village while I go meet him.'

Fear leapt into Cara's eyes. 'Oh, Trent, is that wise? Why not let the men here support you — '

'I can handle him,' he said grimly, envisaging Silver going down under his flaming gun in the starlight. Right now he felt made for this dangerous life. Maybe the slum was reaching out and reclaiming him after all the straight years.

Silver came in casually, seemingly indifferent to any danger that might be present. The dude appeared almost relieved when Trent stepped out from behind a clump of brush with the rifle trained squarely on his chest.

'Drop your irons, Silver!'

The rider reined in. Clanton waited until he'd shucked his weapons without protest before approaching.

'All right, where are the others?' he demanded. 'Wolves always hunt in packs.'

'Sorry, but I'm riding solo today, cowboy,' Silver drawled, sliding to ground. 'You can believe that. Told my pards I had a good lead on you I could follow up faster alone.' He smiled humourlessly. 'And they bought it, but of course brains ain't their long suit. Anything to drink in this pesthole?'

Later, with a mug of sourmash in his fist and one boot propped up on a footstool in the head man's raggedy lodge, the Whiskeyville man glanced about thoughtfully, keen eyes missing nothing.

He was genuinely impressed by Clanton's survival and present set-up, but revealed he had other things on his mind when he eventually began to speak. Silver talked straight, had been thinking that way ever since Mule Hendry died.

He was all through with Whiskeyville, with Horak and his so-called pards, he declared. When he'd parted company with the searchers earlier, it had not been with the intention of pressing on with a one-man search for the escapers, as he'd declared, but simply to drift. The fast gun and Freemont had been pards, as Clanton knew from Freemont's letters. Burk's death had hit the man hard, and now, having just lost dour Mule, he was a man carrying a heavy weight. Horak had killed both, Freemont excusably perhaps, but Hendry the way you'd butcher a dog.

The hardcase paused gloomily, then shrugged and went on.

'Well, just like you folk, I'm free to keep right on travelling now. Mebbe we could ride together until we get clear of the badlands?' he suggested after draining his glass. 'An extra set of guns can't hurt.'

Clanton was considering this when Cara asked after news of her husband.

'You mean you still care, lady?' the outlaw quizzed with a meaningful glance at her hand resting on the seated Clanton's shoulder.

She nodded. 'Of course I do,' she said.

The gunman took another thoughtful

sip and leaned back with a sigh.

'Well, mebbe if you do care . . . then could be the best thing I can do is keep my mouth shut.'

Cara rose from her kneeling position alongside Clanton's chair. 'What do you mean by that remark, Mr Silver?'

'Yeah,' Trent said sharply. 'What?'

Silver shrugged and talked straight. He had no reason to do otherwise now. Blake had shown up right on time, demanding to see his wife before entering into any discussion of ransom demands, he revealed bluntly. Without letting on that Cara had escaped, Horak had insisted that as a prerequisite to any deal to 'release' her, Blake must draft a personally coded message for transmission to the army post from Taloga, ordering the immediate withdrawal of all troops currently involved in the desert.

'You see,' he went on, his audience stunned, 'Moran and Quent were already in town. Horak wanted to give them his big surprise about the Army deal to fire them up into burying the hatchet, then help form up a mining combine with one another and Whiskeyville. And then the biggest prize of all — have the big men throw in with us and start mining out in the Funerals.'

He paused and spread his hands.

'This sounded just fine to everybody. Only your old man wasn't aiming to order anyone anyplace until he saw with his own eyes that you were alive and unharmed, ma'am.'

The outlaw's eyes crinkled at the corners as they flicked from Trent to Cara.

'Seems to me that sojer might be a country mile hotter for you than you are for him, if you don't mind me saying so, lady.'

'Cut that talk,' rapped Clanton.

'Make me,' Silver flared. He might be played out and disarmed, yet remained what he had always been. Tough enough.

'My husband — ' Cara began urgently but Silver cut her off impatiently.

'He had Horak on the spot, your old

207

man did. We couldn't produce you, couldn't let him know you'd flown the coop. But Horak will force him to authorize that order to Army HQ now, no matter how tough Blake reckons he is. Yessir, the colonel will end up giving him that code . . . even if the boys have to put out his eyes or slow-roast him over a barbecue.'

Cara's hand flew to her mouth. 'Matthew is being tortured?'

'Sure enough. But I'll give that stiff-necked soldier his due. He is a country mile tougher than he looks. They might be drawing sweat and blood out of him, but that was all they're getting when I quit town.'

Silver glanced about.

The room was suddenly very quiet.

He held up his empty glass but nobody responded.

'I don't get it,' he said, heaving out of the chair to go for the bottle himself. 'You dumped him, lady, and Clanton here cuckolded him, or so I've been told. Now you're both acting like the colonel was your bestest old buddy.'

He filled his glass and held it high.

'To best buddies past and present,' he said just a little thickly. 'Freemont . . . yeah, we could start with him, eh, Clanton? Your best friend and surely one of mine. Then there's the colonel . . . nobody's best buddy by the look of things here . . . not even yours, Miz Blake, but surely some kinda hero. And now, last but not least, a final 'So-long old-timer' to good old Mule, my pard sent West 'way ahead of time by Horak, the mongrel dog bastard. Bottoms up!'

The boozy toast was ignored by a sober Clanton and Cara. But they could not ignore the impact of Silver's words which seemed to carry the chilling ring of truth. Their gazes interlocked as though they could read each other's thoughts as plain as day.

★　★　★

Everyone paused to stare as Horak entered the barroom, bootheels cracking loud.

He even succeeding in intimidating portly Hud Moran and spare-bodied Luke Quent. These kings of grass castles had been lured here by the dream of riches which each now believed was attainable, yet still found themselves uneasy in their new partner's company.

While Whiskeyville looked on, fascinated and unsure.

It was impossible to keep secret what was happening here today. Copper-talk was in the air and just about every booze-addled derelict low-rent pimp-thief nursed his own feverish dreams of Kaw Hill and the metal that had always been there but which it had been too dangerous for any to go after. Until now, maybe — if rumours were true.

For a time the town had thought Horak was at last going to make it big. But whatever his grand plan had been, it had surely sprung a leak earlier when Trent Clanton got to gun down the Dancer then vanished with Horak's all-important hostage.

But they still believed 'the big fella'

would come out on top. He always did.

Until that actually happened, however, nobody would really feel free to relax and throw a big celebration to mark the successful outcome of the big-bill event, WHISKEYVILLE VS THE ARMY!

Horak sneered at them. He looked the most confident man in the desert yet he was walking on broken glass right now. Without Blake's authority to Fort Comstock not to attempt his rescue, nothing was safe here for Horak and his new partners. Yet Blake was still holding out against the grisly maestro of pain Vinnie Gascoigne. What was that bluebelly made of? Cement?

But of course if they found the wife it would simply be a matter of presenting her before her husband with a stiletto at her throat and Blake would snap like a dead stick.

So near and yet so far.

Whiskey hit the bartop before Horak reached it. He propped to glare a question at Moran and Quent, whose men had joined the hunt for the runners hours earlier.

'No luck,' Moran said with a windy sigh. 'The boys ain't found nary a sign of that pair noplace.'

'Noplace,' affirmed Moran, red-faced and chafing but still an imposing figure with fat pink jowls and a jaw like John Henry's hammer. 'Seems to us that Freemont's kid character might be as smart at trail-blotting as he is at . . .'

He bit off the words. But he had gone too far.

'As good as he is at making jaspers like us look idiots?' Horak said ominously. He made a vicious gesture. 'Or as good at dry-gulching good boys like Dandy? That good? Why don't you say it?'

His voice cut and his eyes glared dangerously, yet he didn't go on with it. He mustn't. He couldn't afford another bust-out.

He reached for his drink and caught Gila studying him with that penetrating one-eyed look he hated.

'Want to lose a second eye?' he hissed.

Gila simply vanished, scuttling off along his escape passage, convinced more than ever tonight that at long last his nerves had grown too ragged for this job in this town.

The whiskey tasted sour. But Horak knew it was only him. He headed for the doors and strode out into the moaning night to double-check on the guard, his torturers, anything to burn up the energy and escape those questioning stares. If he never took off another trophy, this was the event he simply had to win. It was the biggest and therefore the best.

He continued beating his way round the almost deserted streets under a low sky, defying the cutting dust-wind on a night you wouldn't let your dog out in, staring out at the darkness as if it was the enemy.

The night stared back.

★　★　★

'I reckoned I'd seen it all,' said Silver, the wind snatching the words from his lips as his buckskin swung its hindquarters into it. 'Jokers gunning down their own pards, plans and schemes too big to pull off, even ramrods showing up like sixgun heroes and riding off with the damsel in distress. But until tonight I never saw a fool on horseback, name of Silver — a man with no reason on God's earth to want to die — so damnfool eager to get himself killed, and for no good reason. Can anyone riddle me the why of that?'

'I suggest you decided to return with us to Whiskeyville because you are a finer man than you want to admit, Mr Silver,' returned Cara, sheepskin collar turned up high about her face, voice barely audible as the gusts came stronger again. The outlaw grimaced as a greasewood bough bent low and almost dislodged his hat. He clamped it on tight and glanced sideways at Clanton, who was watching the town ahead like a predator.

'What's your theory, Freemont's kid? You reckon I'm just out to get square over what happened to old Mule, but just don't want to admit it?'

'Where are those glasses of yours?' was Trent's only response. Silver drew the item from his saddlebags and tossed it across.

'Just let me know if you see anything I should know about!' he yelled. Silver had kept drinking throughout the trio's return journey to the alkali step outside Whiskeyville. He was far from sober yet still seemed sharp and alert.

Sheltered some by a stand of threshing cotton-woods, with the glasses clapped to his eyes, Clanton scanned for look-outs. As if reading his intentions, Silver brought his cayuse closer. He pointed with a long left arm.

'Try over yonder by O'Leary's barn,' he suggested. 'Then the white adobe, the far side by the bone pile and then a hundred yards right of that . . . that corral you can just see over Deane's roof. That's where we set up look-outs

215

if we reckon we might be jumped by redskins or bluebellies. And you can believe me — Horak'll have them all posted tonight. Bet on it.'

By the time he had identified half-hidden figures at three of the four designated points, Trent had reason to be doubly grateful for Silver's presence. Without him he would likely have no chance of infiltrating and rescuing Blake. Even with help, the odds against them seemed tight enough to knot his intestines hard as oakwood.

'Where've they got the colonel?' he asked, still scanning.

'The barn. Tramp and Gascoigne like plenty of room to work in when they set about persuading some prospector to tell where their poke is hid.' Silver glanced at the woman. 'You should be prepared for the worst, ma'am. Those boys play it hard — '

'Someone's moving around in the open out there,' Clanton broke in. 'Across town between that big old black tree and the creek. See! There he goes.'

216

'Give me them glasses.'

Silver took a long look then lowered the instrument with a curse.

'Horak, of course. Seen him do this sort of thing before. Can't relax, and being round people too much when things are tight gets him mad.' He took another look. 'He's gone now. Well, that makes three to four sentries to slip, and Horak liable to pop up behind us any tick of the clock. Still keen, cowboy? I reckon if old Freemont was here he'd rate these odds too steep for a tenderfoot and a drunk.'

'And he would be right,' Trent replied, hauling a sixgun to check it out. 'Which is why we're going to leave our horses yonder at that old shack with Cara, then move in real quiet down there by the sump and start in cutting down the odds. What do you want? The barn and the colonel, or the sentries?'

'Remind me about Mule again,' Silver said slowly, uncapping his brown bottle with pensive deliberation as they moved the horses cautiously on.

'Horak murdered him in cold blood.'

'Good, I needed that to stiffen my spine.' The outlaw drank and stoppered the bottle with the heel of his hand. 'OK, I'll take Horak and the sentries. Some of those good old boys could've helped Mule if they'd wanted. But you could find more than two at the barn, you know?'

'I know it.'

'How come you ain't running scared, Clanton?'

'I'm scared. I'm just not running.'

10

WILD NIGHT IN WHISKEYVILLE

The colonel's eyes were shut tight. They hurled a bucket of water into his face but he would not open his eyes. Fierce pain bolted up his right arm from his hand as a sliver was forced deeper beneath the fingernail. His hair felt it was standing on end, yet Colonel Matthew Blake's lips remained tightly compressed and no sound escaped him. He was blotting everybody out, was struggling to blot out the pain along with them.

A fist crashed against his cheekbone and he actually smiled.

They had been working on him for many hours now. He looked like hell yet showed no sign of weakening. To him, that wild blow and the curse that accompanied it indicated that his torturers were growing frustrated, were maybe beginning at last to suspect that he might never cave in.

The longer it went on the stronger he seemed to grow. For each passing hour cemented a suspicion bordering on certainty now that they didn't have his wife to hold over his head, as he'd first feared. Reason told him that if they were holding her they would have brought her before him, when he knew he'd have cracked wide open and given them what they wanted before letting them hurt her. He would never submit to Horak's demands now. He was too much a soldier for that.

He was struck again and the colonel welcomed the darkness of unconsciousness. Hawk-faced Tramp massaged his knuckles and turned his back on the battered figure sagging from straps attached to the barn's sturdy centre pole. He hawked and cursed, glancing nervously towards the doors. There was no telling when Horak would show again. The only certainty was that he would come, and when he did they'd still have nothing.

'What now?' the outlaw growled at Gascoigne. 'What's left? We've tried everythin' . . . burnin', cuttin', beltin'. I've never seen nothin' like it. The bastard's made of iron.'

'It's all Horak's fault,' Gascoigne said bitterly. 'He underrated Freemont's kid right from the jump, and now he's paying full price for his mistake.'

He suddenly stopped and squared his jaw. 'So are you going to take that iron out of that fire or are we just aiming to stand here wrangling until Kurt stops by and starts in whippin' our asses?'

Peering into the lamp-lit barn through a chink in the wall-planking twenty feet away, Trent Clanton waited until Tramp bent over the brazier fire and Gascoigne reached for his tobacco. Then he eased to the side door and opened it to step inside behind a cocked .45.

Tramp dropped the hot iron and floor straw began to fry. Vinnie Gascoigne froze solid.

'One wrong move and you're dead!' Trent warned, approaching the centre pole. He waved his piece. 'You, Tramp, ditch your irons and untie the colonel. Come on, come on, and if you get any fancy ideas, just think of what happened to Dandy. Move!'

He had them cold.

Blake groaned and stirred when he felt his thongs begin to loosen. Tramp's bony fingers were trembling, but his henchman still wasn't intimidated. Outraged, disbelieving, Gascoigne stood in a crouch like a man actually considering charging down a naked gun at point-blank range.

Blake was free and lurched about in bewilderment. Gascoigne scented a chance when a distant shriek rose above the wind, the sort of cry a man might make with a Bowie driven to the hilt in his body. Either Silver had struck or been struck, Clanton guessed. Either way, all hope of stealth had just evaporated. Vinnie Gascoigne whipped a hand from behind his back to produce a derringer with such blinding speed that the barn reverberated to the lethal little weapon's deadly crack before Trent could get his Colt working.

Gascoigne went over backwards to crash across a bench, where he sagged for a moment until the next bullet knocked him down on to his face.

A flung hot iron rebounded off Trent's shoulder with a fierce kiss of pain, sending him reeling. He grabbed for the upright to steady himself as Tramp dived upon his discarded guns and tried to tear them from the leather. Clanton steadied his gun hand and killed the man the way he would a rattler, the bullet going clear through the skinny body, blasting a grisly spray of lung and liver out through the backbone and leaving the hardcase twitching hideously into the smouldering straw.

Blake was back on his feet by now, but still reeling drunkenly, looking like an animated side of bloodied beef. Trent couldn't believe what savagery the colonel must have gone through as he grabbed his arm, the sounds of uproar rising in the blustery night outside.

Blake fell. Trent was assisting him to his feet when he heard horses plunging to a halt directly outside. He let his man drop and dived for the doors. He'd expected it to take longer for the enemy to reach the barn from the saloon. Nothing for it now but to meet them head on and pray he really was the natural with a Colt that Freemont had always vaunted him to be.

He almost shot Cara as she sprang from her saddle, clutching the leads of the spare horses.

'I knew you would need me here, not out there!' she cried. 'Oh my God, is he — ?'

'Alive, Cara, very much alive!' the colonel rasped, staggering through the doors. 'But in God's name what are you doing here?'

A gunflash chewed a vivid orange hole in the blackness off to one side and something hard smacked the doors with a thud. Next moment a horse went down screaming and Trent knew there would be no escape this time, no flying run-out. They barely made it back inside before the space where they'd been standing was cross-hatched by flying lead.

★ ★ ★

'Splendid shooting, Clanton!' applauded the colonel, peering through a chink in the planking where he saw a running figure somersault then slideskid for yards on his face as the crash of Trent's rifle began to fade. 'Did he catch you?'

Clanton was leaning away from his improvised gunport with one shirtsleeve soaking with blood. Instantly Cara quit reloading guns and rushed to his side, her face wearing an expression her husband had never seen before as she ripped at the shirt and began stanching the wound with the wadded cloth.

And for the first time on this endless

day, Matthew Blake seemed to sag, crumpling inwardly until forced to lean against the scarred old walls for support.

He had been warned, of course. His torturers had taken great delight in claiming that the wife for whom he had been so willing to give up his freedom, career and quite probably his life, had fallen in love with a stranger. That gabby Momma Deane insisted they'd slept together; all attested that the rugged ramrod had transformed himself into a gunfighter-hero to spirit his wife out of town to safety — just like in a romantic novel.

Naturally the colonel had rejected every word right up to the moment he first saw them both together. Then, immediately, he had known. There could be no doubt. He knew his wife better than anyone living, having spent years watching and studying her, waiting desperately to see an expression on her face for him such as there was now for Clanton.

Blake was shattered, but still the soldier. He was back at the wall in an instant, where Clanton rejoined him with his shoulder strapped and rifle in hand.

For what seemed an age the two men stood shoulder to shoulder trading shots with the swift, demonic figures out there in the semi-darkness, before a flying bullet smashed a lantern in the loft which they hadn't had time to extinguish. Instantly the hay was ablaze and the enemy began to howl in triumph. Within mere minutes it was looking desperate for the defenders. Yet before despair could overcome them a sudden storming volley of fresh gunfire, coming from the direction of the rooming-house, triggered off a bedlam of curses and wild cries immediately outside.

Peering out, Trent glimpsed two gunmen staggering from the cover of the corrals, clawing at their bodies in agony as bullets slammed into them from the Deanes' darkened windows.

'Silver!' Clanton gasped. 'It's got to be.' His heart leapt. 'That man's a shooting fool!'

'This plainly affords us the opportunity we've been praying for,' Blake said with brisk urgency as he limped to the small door facing the creek. He beckoned impatiently with one hand and produced a fistful of bullets with the other, his blood-streaked features ghastly in the flame-light. 'Quickly, quickly! I can stand them off indefinitely now they are forced to diversify their attack. When you make the creek you can wade downstream and make your way round behind the corrals to reach the horses. Cara, will you please get a move on?'

'What are you talking about, Matthew?' she gasped. 'We're not leaving without you.'

'Of course you are. In my condition I wouldn't get as far as the first tree . . . '

His voice caught in his throat, faded. Standing there in his agony, he appeared infinitely older than his years, a plain, serious man with his heart in his eyes. And every cut, bruise and burn he displayed gave his wife and the ramrod searing evidence of what this man had been prepared to suffer, both for Cara and to deny evil men what they wanted. 'Besides,' he continued in a different tone, 'you have infinitely more to live for than I . . . both of you.' He shook his head as both made to protest.

'No, I'm neither mistaken nor angry. Plainly you've found the only treasure worth finding, and it would be a sin to throw it away. Just kiss me, Cara, and be on your way.'

For a hanging moment nothing stirred in that smoke-hazed building as three people, drawn together by events beyond their control or even understanding, faced one another and the reality of who they were and exactly what was unfolding.

Everything was crystal-clear for the colonel, who'd made his decision and would stick to it.

But Cara and Trent, without even exchanging a single word, with nothing more than one vivid look, both knew it was the end. Certainly they could run, just as they might well have done at Council Creek. But they hadn't done so then, and could not now, for the self-same reason.

Until an hour earlier Blake had just been a name to Clanton. Now he was a decent and heroic man demonstrating what total devotion could be like. For what greater proof of that could any man offer than by showing willing to sacrifice the one he loved to another.

Others might have seized the opportunity to go, but they did not. They were the last people who should have fallen in love when not free to do so. All their lives, both Trent Clanton and Cara Blake had lived up to a standard. In this unforgettable moment they were suddenly and inescapably reminded of who and what they were, of things that not even love could change.

A bullet slammed through a chink in

the wall and struck the centre support with a smack.

'We can't desert Flint and Slattery,' was Clanton's tight-lipped excuse for staying put. And with just the one agonized glance at Cara's drawn face, he swung away to man his gunport again. Blake protested, but Trent was both unheeding and unhearing. The only reality he was willing to deal with at that moment was the enemy.

*　*　*

'Hey, Kurt!' Silver shouted above the stutter of gunfire. 'You still out there, big man? Or mebbe you're hiding under a hollow log like the yellow dog you've always been?'

The voice carried. It reached into Gila's, where ashen cattle kings sat hunched and trembling behind the guns of their cowboys. Where painted women and ragged men sucked at their drinks wondering if each sip might be their last. And Gila stood behind his bar feigning an indifference to the violence raging outside while feeling so terrified he could scarcely breathe.

The shout was heard in the ramshackle houses of those who lived off the gunmen, rose above the wailing of the women weeping for men who'd already fallen in the murderous gunplay at O'Leary's barn and the Deanes'.

Those responding to the fusillade coming from the roomer where Silver had bluffed, cajoled and even menaced a number of anti-Horak factioners into backing his play and making their own stand, heard the defiant taunt and wondered where Horak might be. The big man had been whipping up the attacks a short time before, but now there was no sign.

But crouched behind a well housing with a bullet-bloodied leg, hawk-faced Kurt was the first to react to the taunting cry: 'God damn Horak anyway! Iffen he hadn't kilt Freemont the way he done that damned cowboy sonuva bastard would never of come here. And if he hadn't gone and plugged old Mule we wouldn't have Johnny shootin' the living crap out of us right now! What are we fighting for, does anybody know?'

That was the beginning.

It had been impossible to resist Horak when in full cry and leading from the front. But with men tumbling all about them now and no sign of the defenders caving in, more and more were beginning to ask themselves what the hell were they dying for, as slowly but surely the rate of their fire began to diminish.

Horak read these signs correctly, as did Trent Clanton. But of the two, only Trent — calm as Freemont had trained him to be — reacted as a real fighting man might. Sprawled upon the roof of the barn he had been scanning the smoke-ghosted town ever since the attack began to falter. He suddenly had his vigilance rewarded when he picked out the familiar silhouette, watching from the bridge.

That was all Horak was doing now.

Watching. He was not afraid — never afraid of the fighting. It was the fear of failure that undercut him now. With everything crumbling before his eyes a vast and raging bitterness gripped his guts.

For he was seeing reality as never before.

The way this whole damn town had turned out for Freemont's funeral should have been a warning to him, he realized now. Then that hick ramrod had ridden all the way from Kansas to honour him, and had sown the seeds against him in Freemont's lousy name. And totally unexpected, Judas Silver had cared enough about Hendry to come back and challenge him here, to challenge them all. Then the woman had fallen for Clanton and the stinking noble colonel had surrendered himself to them in order to save her. There were friendships, cliques, heroism, liaisons and partnerships on every hand even in this shabby town.

But who would grieve if he should

234

fall? Was there even one.

'Killer!'

He whirled. A dim figure was limping across the bridge, smoky light gleaming on the weapon he toted. Horak raised both Colts as he crouched and squinted hard. Then his eyes snapped wide.

Freemont's damned kid!

He'd counted Clanton as good as dead in the barn. How had he got to bust out, circle the bridge and now cut off his run-out?

'We'll end all this right here and now, Horak.' Trent gestured with the gun. 'The whole damn shooting-match. I'm going to kill you the way you killed Burk. And you'll go knowing your boys won't kill me. There's not one of them that'll go on fighting when you're dead.'

Disbelief hit Horak in a tumultuous surge of exhilaration as he realized what a fatal mistake this hick had made. Clanton could have cut him down from behind but instead had opted to make a hero play.

What a fool!

Horak could outgun any cowboy ever born. This would be an execution, not a gunfight. Clanton was the prime enemy and when they saw him fall the traitors and Judases would surely fold. Horak's 'loyal pards' would finish Silver and then he would be back on top — all thanks to one fool of a Kansas cowboy. Without a word his twin guns whipped up and Clanton's breath caught at his speed. Yet he was only a fraction behind, and Freemont was with him one last time as he stood firm to take one bullet in the thigh then another raking his ribs.

'Better to be straight than fast,' he whispered aloud and fired just once. The big figure before him seemed to freeze solid. Unable to trigger, breathe, or even to fall, Horak stood there incredulous and silent until the ragged wind gusted and blew him over, his going a soft rustle against the earth.

★　★　★

Trent turned away from Freemont's grave at the sound of horses. They were coming up the low rise from the town along the north-east trail, twenty men all in military blue escorting the coach, with more troopers riding behind the rig.

The colonel had come alone to Whiskeyville but today he was leading the way the commanding officer of Fort Comstock should. There was even a trooper holding the regimental standard high, and Trent grinned when he saw Sergeant Flint, one stiff leg sticking out, riding side by side with Trooper Slattery behind the coach.

A further squad of soldiers was left in town to complete the mopping up, and even cynics like Gila were now predicting that the culling of Whiskeyville's hardcases and the tenuous but hopeful pact between the two big ranchers would bring at last a kind of peace to the desert — thanks almost entirely and unintentionally to the ruthless ambition of just one man who now lay nearby in an unmarked grave.

He sobered as the vanguard of mounted men went by. The couple sat side by side in the coach and Trent returned Blake's salute. He looked into her face for the last time and her farewell glance would warm him for a long long time to come.

OK, so Trent Clanton was alone again. Back to Kansas and the ranch. Buck Foster had heard all about the gun battle and had sent a message pleading with him to come back to his old job before his wild cowboys ruined him and put him in his grave. Back to the routine life of a ranch ramrod, the steady money, the good times, the meaningless flirtations. After twenty-five years alone he had at last found the one woman whom he could love — who loved him — and he had let her go.

So why did he feel almost good as the last saluting cavalryman clattered by him as he stood tall and straight there against the backdrop of headstones and summer-yellowed grasses?

Maybe it was because he understood the inevitability and rightness of it all, or perhaps it could be the comfort he found in his vision.

He leaned on his cane and gazed into the future. Cara would always be a good wife now, as she had always been meant to be. Blake had never been able to show his true devotion for her until presented with that opportunity by Horak the killer. She might never love her husband with the fierceness she had shown Trent, but he doubted either of them would even notice. She would be the perfect officer's lady, would possibly bear him his children, might even live her later years in some place like Boston or Washington where Blake would accept some diplomatic post.

She would have all of that and he would play no part in it. But Cara and Trent would always have Whiskeyville.

She'd set him free of his brutal past

and taught him he could love; he knew now he would love again.

But until he did . . .

He slid his hand inside his coat to touch his chest. They shared the same heartbeat. So how could he ever be alone again?

He limped towards the gatepost where the horse was tied, yet his gait was almost jaunty.

It was two hundred miles to Kansas.

THE END

We do hope that you have enjoyed reading this large print book.

Did you know that all of our titles are available for purchase?

We publish a wide range of high quality large print books including:
Romances, Mysteries, Classics
General Fiction
Non Fiction and Westerns

Special interest titles available in large print are:
The Little Oxford Dictionary
Music Book, Song Book
Hymn Book, Service Book

Also available from us courtesy of Oxford University Press:
Young Readers' Dictionary
(large print edition)
Young Readers' Thesaurus
(large print edition)

For further information or a free brochure, please contact us at:
Ulverscroft Large Print Books Ltd.,
The Green, Bradgate Road, Anstey,
Leicester, LE7 7FU, England.
Tel: (00 44) **0116 236 4325**
Fax: (00 44) **0116 234 0205**

Other titles in the
Linford Western Library:

THE HIDDEN APACHES

Mike Stall

Phil Roche, the foremost gambler on the Mississippi riverboats, was an exacting man. To cheat him and live, you had to be quicker on the draw. So far nobody had been. But all that changed when he heard that Susan had been murdered and her child, Lucie, kidnapped. The Apaches seemed to be the prime suspects. Now the people of Lanchester County would discover that Roche could be just as tough outside the casino. But his search for Lucie uncovers more than he had bargained for . . .